MAEVE

JOSIE RIVIERA

PRAISE AND AWARDS

USA TODAY bestselling author

5 STAR REVIEWS

InD'Tale Magazine Review:

"Who wouldn't want to spend a week in Corsica, all expenses paid? Maeve Doherty might not. She is a spunky Irish lass who works for a hotel chain and lives paycheck to paycheck. She has to, since she's taking care of her younger brother, who has cancer. When she discovers she's been chosen to go on a week-long vacation with a man who some computer program has decided is her "Perfect Match," she almost says no.

Edward Newell, a London businessman, owns a lucrative hotel chain and lives a life of luxury, flying around the world in his private jet. From the start, two facts are clear: Maeve and Edward come from two entirely different social and economic worlds, and they have one trait in common: they are both "married to their jobs," so neither intends to marry.

With its "Bachelorette" theme, the author's colorful prose and detailed descriptions are delightful to read.

The chemistry between the two and the development of Edward's character are excellently done. This sweet romance is a quick read that takes the reader on an all-expense-paid vacation in a dreamily romantic setting."

"What a great way to end the Perfect Match series! I loved the story, the setting, the characters - all of it! Maeve was kind and unselfish. Edward was charming and a gentleman.Their first meeting made me laugh! They definitely had the chemistry, but I appreciated the fact that it was all of the other things that really brought them together. There were so many wonderful moments, and a great ending!" -**Amazon Reviewer**

"A very touching story about a single mother. I found the book to be very inspirational in the context. A great book to read! Maeve may be thePerfect Match Book 6 but it is the second book in the series for me to read. Josie Riviera gives us a heroine in desperate need of a vacation.She is also in need of a perfect match, so I was cheering her on all the way. Of course, her match turns out to be someone just as driven as she is. I liked Maeve more so than Edward.

I loved this story and couldn't put it down and I hope you find this book as enjoyable as I did." -**Bookbub Reviewer**

INTRODUCTION

To keep up on newly released ebooks, paperbacks, Large Print Paperbacks, audiobooks, as well as exclusive sales, sign up for Josie's Newsletter today.

As a thank you, I'll send you a Free PDF ... The Beauty Of ...

Josie's Newsletter

Did you know that according to a Yale University study, people who read books live longer?

This book is dedicated to all my wonderful readers who have supported me every inch of the way.

THANK YOU!

PROLOGUE

$\mathcal{M}$aeve's Perfect Match Dating Profile ...
Miss Irish Independence, Age 26

THE QUOTE *that best defines me is from the French singer Edith Piaf's "Le Vie en rose," that when a man takes her in his arms, she sees the world through rose-colored glasses.*

I LIVE *for a hot cuppa tea and will share it with you.*

I'm a good listener. But make no mistake, I follow my own dreams, not yours.

Love comes in many forms, and I believe in a commitment to one person.

BE WARNED ... *I'm a workaholic.*

CHAPTER 1

"*I*t'll do you good to get away from Ireland. We've had a rainy summer."

"Rainy summer?" Maeve Doherty grinned at her best friend, Colleen O'Keefe, who was busily swiping Maeve's phone. "When can you recall a non-wet summer in Ireland?"

"A year ago. It was on a Thursday."

Maeve laughed out loud. As always, her flaming-haired friend's sunny disposition lifted her spirits.

Colleen chuckled in return. Her tailored canary-yellow pantsuit, with matching pumps, fit her full-figured body impeccably. Maeve glanced at her own worn linen skirt and smoothed her wrinkled polyester blouse. When had she last taken time for herself? She'd forgotten, it had been so long ago, with all the worry and sleepless nights.

Colleen plunked into an oversized chair in the lobby of the building that housed the Merrimac Company. The women were purchasing agents for a small Irish hotel chain. Their duties included placing orders for everything from hotel furniture to cleaning supplies, and comparing various prices and the quality of the merchandise.

Colleen pointed with one of her French manicured fingernails at Maeve's phone screen. "If I'm reading this email correctly, you've been offered a free week at the paradise island of your choice, compliments of the Perfect Match dating agency."

Maeve pulled up a chair across from her friend. "Aye."

Keeping her fingertip on the blinking cursor, Colleen paused. "You plan to accept, don't you?"

"Whatever the catch is, it's not worth a week anywhere on the globe."

"This offer is from Amy Yates, your friend from America, and her husband, Dawson. And it's a personalized invitation." Colleen scanned Maeve's phone screen. "A free vacation, a romantic getaway, a chance—"

Maeve held up a hand. "Aye."

"So it's legit," Colleen declared gaily. "I remember you said they owned the agency."

"Aye."

"Which island are you choosing?"

"I'm not choosing any island because I'm not going."

"How about Corsica, France?" Colleen obviously pretended she hadn't heard Maeve. "You've always wanted to learn French. And isn't there a famous museum there you've always wanted to visit?"

"Maison Bonaparte, the ancestral home of the Bonaparte family." Maeve nodded. "The museum is located in Ajaccio, Corsica."

"Then go."

"Yes, someday, on my own, using my own money—not obligated to a matchmaking agency."

Colleen pushed her glasses up her nose and peered at the phone. "All expenses are paid and the terms and conditions are clearly spelled out. All you have to do is agree to spend

4

the week with your match or risk being charged for the vacation."

Maeve lifted a skeptical eyebrow. "That's all?"

"It's a massive marketing campaign to introduce their new business," Colleen reminded her. "You're helping them as much as they're helping you."

"I love history, but I'm not that desperate to see Napoléon Bonaparte's death mask. I'd prefer spending a cozy week in my flat reading a pile of European history books." Maeve tapped her fingers together and drew in a breath. "Figure in a hot cuppa Irish tea and lemon scones from The Ground Café and I'll be merry as a leprechaun."

"You're emotionally spent," her friend said quietly. "And you gave Amy Yates permission to plug your name into the Perfect Match database."

Maeve turned a despairing look on Colleen. "Aye, in a flash of desperation when I feared any opportunity for love was passing me by. I'm over that."

Was she?

Once she'd recovered from the sadness and shock of learning her twenty-year-old brother Owen had been diagnosed with cancer, she'd settled into the daily task of tending to him when he opted to move in with her rather than live with their mother. She'd given up every pastime she enjoyed to care for him, including auditioning for minor acting roles, something she loved.

Now that Owen's radiation treatments were over and his caregiving routine had become stable, perhaps she could ease up a bit, take a breather. Perhaps …

"Maeve?" Colleen prodded. "Owen is in remission and he can go live with your mother for a week. She's able-bodied and can tend to him. You're only twenty-six. Live your life."

"Most days my mother isn't capable of washing a dish, let

alone attending to a sick adult. She had a hard-enough time being a parent when Owen was well."

"Your mother lands in the middle of drama because of the type of men she sees, and her ongoing dilemmas can't always be your problem." Colleen leaned back in her chair. Her normally keen bright-blue gaze softened. "Enough about your mother. What's the craic with you? Are you sleeping okay?"

Maeve shrugged. "I'm always tired, although everyone is exhausted nowadays because of our hectic lifestyles."

"Grab this chance. Go. Believe me, if it weren't for my boyfriend, Colin, I'd take your place."

Colleen and Colin had an on-again, off-again relationship that had lasted for over a year. Currently, it was on again.

A reassuring grin crossed Colleen's freckled face. "Along with Owen's healthcare providers, your mother will mind him brilliantly. I want to see an optimistic smile on your face again. I'm sure you'll have a lorry-load of stories to share when you get back."

Maeve shook her head. "Because of all the days I missed when Owen became ill, I'm on the verge of losing my job. I certainly can't afford to take off any more time. Besides, his medical bills are mounting, and our private insurance only covers part of them."

"You're physically and mentally exhausted. *Your* health is important too. You need the time away to maintain your sense of balance."

"Aye, perhaps," Maeve admitted. Her brother's cancer journey had been a lengthy road crowded with difficult decisions and the challenges of radiation treatment.

"The Merrimac Company wants to branch out of Ireland and explore resort areas for other hotels. Pitch the idea to our manager. Tell Mrs. McShea it's a working holiday. Just think you'll get paid for sitting on a beach in a bikini."

"I don't swim, and I've never worn a bikini."

"Live a wee bit, Maeve. Spend your days lying in a lounge chair and looking out at the Mediterranean. You once told me there are over two hundred beaches in Corsica. Imagine the sun, the surf—"

"Colleen—"

"The sand." Colleen laughed. "It's a win-win. Besides, who can pass up the chance to meet Mr. Right?"

"I'm too busy to fritter away my valuable time on a man. And there's no such man as Mr. Right, at least not for me."

"How do you know? Make the time."

"Suppose he's not interesting?"

"Suppose he is?"

"What about Crinkles?"

"Your dog is accustomed to your ma's flat." Colleen tapped the phone screen again. "Amy says her agency's matchmaking algorithms are the best and they're launching this campaign to prove it."

"And if you keep scrolling, you'll see they want people who've been unlucky in love."

Like her.

Maeve studied Merrimac's lobby—a gleaming brown floor, mahogany table, anything but her friend's sympathetic stare. She'd spilled out more than she'd intended.

A year ago while visiting a cousin in America, she'd met Amy while shopping in an exclusive boutique, not realizing at first that she was chatting with the owner of the boutique. They'd become instant friends, and they shared coffee and heartfelt conversation after the store closed. That evening, Maeve had poured out her sadness to her new-found confidante.

Finbar, Maeve's boyfriend of two years, had broken up with her—not even in person—but through a dismissive text.

"No more," she'd declared to Amy. "Men and their hollow promises are not to be believed."

Wasn't Maeve's father, who'd left her mother without an explanation, further proof of her statement? He'd said he'd return. He never had.

"Maeve? Maeve?" Colleen yanked Maeve from her upsetting remembrances. "I'm partial to the final line of your dating profile." She read aloud: "'Love comes in many forms, and I believe in a commitment to one person.' Colleen looked up at Maeve. "Aww, that's very sweet. You expressed yourself perfectly."

Heat rose in Maeve's face. "I'm starry-eyed and foolish for writing something so reckless. No one stays with one person forever."

"Some do. Some people have a love that lasts. Where are those rose-colored glasses you used to wear?"

"I've put them away and become realistic."

"Dust them off. What if Mr. Right is waiting for you in Corsica?"

"He won't be, although just to be sure ..." Maeve grabbed her phone from Colleen and included another line at the bottom of her dating profile.

Be warned ... I'm a workaholic.

Colleen squinted at the screen. "Being a workaholic is supposed to deter him?"

"I'll plead nine-to-five obligations."

Plus, any other excuses necessary to safeguard her heart.

"So, it's settled." Colleen flashed a quick smile. "You'll accept Amy's offer and choose Corsica."

"Aye." Maeve feigned enthusiasm, then blew out a breath.

She'd go, she'd rest, she'd work. But she wouldn't risk falling in love.

Once was enough. Besides, if there was a perfect match

for her on God's emerald-green planet, she'd have found him by now in Ireland.

"That's grand," Colleen said. "Finally, you're doing something for yourself." With a flourish, Colleen stood and walked over to Maeve, throwing her arms around her. "Get ready, my dear friend, for an amazing adventure!"

CHAPTER 2

*E*dward Newell arrived in Corsica aboard his family's private jet. He'd initially flown from London to Nice, where he'd spent the night so he could check on a family-owned resort property. From there, he'd flown on to Corsica, an easy forty-five-minute trip.

The Perfect Match agency had offered to arrange his travel; he'd declined.

Bidding the limo driver, a thank you and farewell, he strode into the marbled lobby of La Bonaparte Resort, pausing to admire wall hangings that depicted Corsica's famed cliffs and its nature reserves. He passed a scattering of loud tourists and headed toward the reception desk.

In a reasonably short while he was greeted by a skinny, clean-shaven man. His tawny-colored hair was raised and swept to the side, giving him a James Dean appearance.

"*Bonjour, monsieur.* My name is Pierre Martin, and I'm the head concierge. Please allow me to welcome you this Sunday afternoon to our resort." Pierre extended his hand for a shake, then produced a flute of champagne and a cool lavender-scented washcloth.

"Good afternoon." Edward accepted the washcloth and refused the champagne. He drank on rare celebratory occasions, and this wasn't one of them.

"Your name, monsieur?"

"Edward Newell."

Cheerful and energetic, Pierre clicked on his computer while briefing Edward on the hotel's amenities and Wi-Fi. "Ah, you're staying for *une semaine, oui?*"

"One week. That's the plan."

"We hope you enjoy your stay with us." Pierre boasted a reedy French accent and a broad grin. "If you need anything, please don't hesitate to call on my services."

"A glass of iced tea sounds good."

"I'll send it straight to your suite, along with today's newspaper."

"No paper. I can catch up on the news tomorrow."

"Excellent." Pierre typed into his computer and then reached behind the desk. "May I also present your Perfect Match?" He kept his face bland although Edward detected a slight raising of Pierre's carefully tended eyebrows.

"*Merci.*" Edward placed the washcloth on the counter, stuffed the sealed envelope into the inner pocket of his tweed suit jacket, then pulled out his wallet. "Here's a little something—"

"*Non*, monsieur, I don't accept tips. Always my pleasure." He glanced at Edward's woven leather bag and matching briefcase. "Do you need assistance with your luggage?"

A bellhop appeared before Pierre finished his question.

"No, I can manage," Edward said.

"But of course. The young lady … your match … hasn't arrived yet. Her flight from Dublin was delayed."

Dublin. The woman hailed from Ireland? Probably pale-skinned and frail. She'd be sun-burned within fifteen minutes in this blasting heat.

Edward gazed out the floor-to-ceiling windows that stretched across the far end of the hotel. Picture-worthy, the three-tiered infinity pool appeared to collide with the turquoise waters of the Mediterranean.

"I'll alert you when the lady arrives," Pierre was saying. "I'm sure you're anxious to meet her. Mr. and Mrs. Yates arranged a dinner date for you and your match this evening."

"Who are the Yateses?"

"The owners of Perfect Match, monsieur."

"Right." Edward dismissed this fact with an absent wave of his hand. How could he forget? Perhaps he needed this getaway more than he'd figured. As vice president of his father's luxury hotel chain, he was responsible for steering the family fortune in the resort industry's fast-moving climate. If only he had twenty-five hours in a day instead of twenty-four.

He checked his cellphone. He was expecting an important business call from his sister Karen—who was in charge of operations—regarding another acquisition. Briefly, he frowned, noting she hadn't rung yet. She'd probably gotten caught up in her investigation. Her current husband's illicit liaisons, although elusive, had been a source of upset for her and the entire family and she was attempting to find enough proof to end the marriage.

With a sigh, he stepped back and took in the ornateness of the lobby. A trickling fountain, showy-blue sofas and scores of dense-green houseplants created a restful ambiance. He particularly liked the touch of tropical fish swimming in the two-story aquarium. Perhaps his next resort property could feature ...

No, no, no. He needed to think of something other than business. He needed to allow himself time to unwind.

Pierre spoke to him, drawing his attention from the hypnotic aquarium. "May I also mention les Calanche Cliffs are nearby, monsieur? They are world renowned." Pierre displayed a mouthful of white teeth, smiling as if he were imparting the most exciting announcement of his career. He'd obviously been well-schooled in the art of hotel service.

"Very good." Absently, Edward checked his cell phone again.

"And dinner will be served at eight o'clock on our terrace overlooking the sea."

"Then I'll meet this Perfect Match woman at dinner. No need to alert me of her arrival ahead of time."

Pierre raised an eyebrow in seeming approval. "We'll keep the special unveiling of your match a surprise then, oui?"

Edward inclined his head but couldn't help his grimace. "By all means."

He didn't like surprises. This one couldn't be helped.

Pierre tended to folding the washcloth on the counter, politely ignoring Edward's lack of enthusiasm. "Will that be all, monsieur?"

Edward hung back. He'd acted curt to the friendly concierge. To make amends he offered, "Those cliffs you mentioned …"

Pierre brightened. "Les Calanche Cliffs."

"Are they conducive for hiking?"

"Oui. Miles and miles of trails. The entire island features numerous activities, both tamed and untamed."

"Excellent." Edward grabbed his luggage. "I'm an outdoorsman."

Pierre handed him two keys. "One is for the pool and gym space," he explained. "The other is for your suite, number 201A. Take the elevator or staircase on your left."

Edward turned away. "*Merci*, Pierre. Cheers."

"May you find your true love in our one-of-a-kind paradise," Pierre called after him, loud enough for the entire lobby to overhear.

Edward swiveled. At his raised eyebrows, Pierre explained, "Mr. Yates's words, monsieur, not mine."

With a succinct nod, Edward turned away again, but then he lingered, his gaze fixed on a pair of cardinal tetras swimming in the aquarium. A host of other tropical fish in neon colors, silvers and stripes, swam alongside.

An all-expense-paid holiday in stunning Corsica wasn't the reason he was here, and he was tempted to tell Pierre that. Nor was it to find the woman of his dreams, as if such a woman existed.

He pursed his lips together and blew out a long breath.

To his knowledge, his two younger adult brothers had never experienced love, that warm, tingly sensation that prompted besotted men to write poems and become blind to common sense. And his sister was certainly nowhere near genuine love in her married life. Only their parents seemed to have found it, their time-tested marriage having lasted thirty years.

Briefly, he considered strangling his friend Bentley for setting him up for this promotion. Bentley was in the hotel business also, although lately Edward had heard that Bentley's business had dipped, largely due to being nudged out by competitors' renovated hotels and absentee ownership. The fact was, Bentley was never around. He preferred partying and spending any profits.

At any rate, this Perfect Match prank was characteristic of Bentley, always out for a laugh at someone else's expense. But what had started as a practical joke had quickly ballooned into two demands from Edward's entrepreneurial father when he'd gotten wind of the news.

Demand one: Edward was to stake out Corsica for any available property to build another family-owned resort, preferably on a beach. Demand two: Edward was advised to seriously consider making Davinia DeVito, an Italian clothing-line heiress he'd been dating, his wife.

"Settle down, get married. A man needs stability in his life," his father had fussed. "Marriage is what your late mother wanted for you, not you off philandering with every attractive woman in England."

He wasn't philandering, he'd wanted to tell his father. He was simply enjoying his twenties, and now his thirties.

Despite the lush surroundings of La Bonaparte Resort and its breathtaking view of Bonifacio, the old town in the distance, reservations about agreeing to this Perfect Match escapade were growing more well-founded by the minute. And any hopes that this pint-sized island was undiscovered had been dashed by the heavy traffic and congestion he'd experienced on his ride from the airport.

Glancing back at the reservation desk, Edward noted Pierre still observed him, albeit discreetly. A well-trained concierge who could double as a mind reader was an asset to any hotel, but they were sometimes a little too ... curious. With a final nod in Pierre's direction, Edward climbed the stairs, found his suite, and swung open the heavy door.

Outstanding. Posh and proper, decorated in creams and golds and navy blues, with gleaming natural light streaming through the windows. The suite boasted a living room, efficiency kitchen, large bedroom, and a bath with a raised marbled tub. Bottles of chilled mineral water and vases of orange lilies enhanced the sense of privilege.

He loosened his silk tie and set his luggage and briefcase near the cream-colored couch, decorated with throw pillows in rich tapestry.

A crystal bowl piled high with ripe peaches sat artfully on the coffee table alongside a glass of iced tea, sliced lemons and cubes of sugar. Somehow, an invisible employee had reached Edward's room before he'd finished climbing the stairs.

He drained the tea, snagged a peach and unlocked the French doors leading to a railed balcony that held a wrought iron table and chairs. In the center of the table sat a terra-cotta vase brimming with tiny purple blooms.

He slid the vase aside, relaxed on a checkered pillowed chair and took a bite of the peach. The flowers' fragrances and the salty sea scented the air, the peach was tangy and flavorful, and for the first time in months his muscles untightened.

He shrugged off his suit jacket, draped it on the other chair, and closed his eyes. After a quick shower, he'd take an invigorating swim.

And then he'd meet his Perfect Match ...

Right, a bit of a damp squib.

He swallowed and shook his head. Anyone who knew him would vouch that he wasn't husband material. And after dessert this evening, he'd present his side of the equation to the Perfect Match lady, before she pegged him out as the passport to remedy her no-doubt desperate marital status.

All the same, he grabbed the Perfect Match envelope from his jacket pocket and unsealed it.

The opening information stated he and the woman were meeting at eight for dinner. He already knew that thanks to the ever-efficient Pierre.

He unfolded the second sheet and read her profile:

MISS IRISH INDEPENDENCE, *Age 26*

The quote that best defines me is from the French singer Edith Piaf's "Le Vie en rose," that when a man takes her in his arms, she sees the world through rose-colored glasses.

I live for a hot cuppa tea and will share it with you.

I'm a good listener. But make no mistake, I follow my own dreams, not yours.

Love comes in many forms, and I believe in a commitment to one person.

BE WARNED ... *I'm a workaholic.*

SO SHE WAS INDEED IRISH, and a feisty independent woman. He chuckled. And a type-A personality from the sounds of it. Just like him.

He turned over her photo and his breath caught.

This was her? This woman was Maeve?

Right ... well ...

Her dark eyes held an impish twinkle. Her chestnut-brown hair was pulled away from her face, enhancing high cheekbones and full pink lips. She was stunning, and he hadn't expected that.

He placed her photo on the table, gazing at her for a long while. Then he reread her profile. *I live for a hot cuppa tea and will share it with you. I'm a good listener.*

Perhaps this Perfect Match setup wasn't such a bad idea.

Maybe she loved the outdoors, as he did. Maybe they'd swim every evening after work, climb the cliffs, dine on exotic Corsican cuisine.

There was no obligation to see her again after the week was over, and enjoying life had always been his motto. In fact, he'd written it on his dating profile.

Emboldened by those thoughts, he grabbed his suit jacket and headed inside his suite to take a shower. He might be a workaholic, but he was still a man.

And besides, they both liked tea.

CHAPTER 3

*M*aeve's anticipated five-hour plane trip from Dublin to Corsica had taken ten. After being delayed by inclement weather, the flight was unnervingly bumpy, and she'd lifted a grateful prayer when they landed in Corsica.

She rang her mother, relieved to hear that her brother, Owen, had received encouraging news at his doctor's appointment that morning. The more time that passed, the lower the risk of recurrence. And Owen had been cancer free for over six months.

Feeling, at least for the moment, all was well in the world, she stepped from the black limousine that had picked her up from the airport to bring her to the small town where La Bonaparte Resort was located. The surrounding picturesque region was cited as one of the top ten places to visit in Europe. As she stepped onto the cobblestone street, she lifted her face to the balmy breeze. A bellhop loaded her bags onto a luggage cart, and she followed him up the hotel's stone steps. Three stories high, the exterior boasted a rustic wooden pattern. Like something out of this world, she reflected, with the backdrop of the fiery-red Mediterranean sun setting behind the hotel and les Calanche Cliffs spiraling upward in the distance.

She'd assumed the weather might be blindingly hot on the island, but the climate was decidedly comfortable. She was looking forward to a refreshing shower and an opportunity to change into clean, unwrinkled clothes. Her traveling outfit, a linen navy skirt, white cotton blouse and sensible leather flats, had looked polished and put together when she'd left her flat. Not so much now. Ruefully, she evened out her skirt to look presentable, then started to the check-in desk.

Awe at the lobby's elegance slowed her pace, and she fingered the straps of the monogrammed jute tote she carried.

Was it too late to reconsider this trip?

Most definitely, she decided with a sigh. Even a one night-stay in a boutique hotel boasting Michelin status would cost a fortune in Euros to repay.

She caught a glimpse of a well-heeled tourist shouldering a designer purse. Clearly, a working-class woman like herself didn't belong here, she thought. She pretended to look around, intent on studying the marbled floor for several beats rather than meet the other woman's gaze.

Why, oh, why had she let Colleen talk her into this trip? Her chest tightened just thinking about the week ahead.

While Maeve waited in a short line to check in, the family ahead of her argued among themselves before stomping away from the reception desk, and swearing in Italian.

"Good evening, mademoiselle. You must be Maeve Doherty, oui?" Behind the oak desk, an impeccably-suited, tawny-haired man with a disarming smile welcomed her. He introduced himself as Pierre Martin, the head concierge, and didn't seem at all flustered by the group before her.

"I am Maeve. Aye."

"We've been expecting you. Welcome to our island of paradise."

"We?"

"The entire hotel staff and Perfect Match. And, of course, your date for the week. I've met him and can assure you he's a delightful fellow."

Delightful fellow.

She refrained from gaping at the view of the infinity pool through the resort's expansive rear windows and tried to return Pierre's grin. "That's grand."

She had no photo of her match, no dating profile, her mind feverishly reminded her. What if Amy and Dawson Yates and their Perfect Match specialists had made a mistake, and she and this "delightful fellow" didn't share any mutual interests? She imagined elaborate computers and compli-cated algorithms searching for ... for what? Computers couldn't be trusted on matters of the heart.

But this wasn't a matter of the heart. This was a working holiday.

"You are *tres belle, mademoiselle,*" Pierre said, "and indeed more beautiful than the profile picture Mrs. Yates sent. I'm certain your match will be very pleased." He struck his fingers to his lips with a whoosh, simulating a kiss. "In the meantime, your suite is on the second floor, room 201B, and Nigel will assist you." He nodded to the bellhop leaning against the luggage cart, then handed her an envelope. "Voila! Your Perfect Match, Miss Doherty. And you'll meet him at eight o'clock for dinner on the terrace."

Voila?

"Thank you," she said. As Pierre went on to describe the highlights of the resort, including the gift shop and a coffee bar, the outdoor pool and a five-star restaurant, she inspected the envelope. Everything vital to accomplish her stay, all the information about her match, was enclosed. This was her week to enjoy herself ... to ease toward relaxation with a man she'd never met.

A few hours spent with him? Aye.

A week?

What would they possibly have in common?

On a half laugh, she debated tearing open the envelope and reading his profile aloud, but didn't want to appear too anxious. Still, her hand shook as she stowed the envelope into her red tote.

Breathe, she chided herself. She'd agreed to the offer and to be spotlighted in promotional publications. She'd redeemed her coupon. She'd signed in good faith, and an Irishwoman stood by her word.

"Pierre, are there any more towels?" a deep male voice called from behind her.

Maeve pivoted and almost collided with a dripping wet man striding to the reception counter. He wore little more than a very tight, very revealing spandex bathing suit. Barefoot, he'd tossed a towel over his shoulders. Water puddled at his feet.

"Mr. Newell." Pierre's eyes widened. The implacable concierge dashed from behind his desk and pitched himself in front of Maeve. "Your match has arrived."

"The Irish woman?" Mr. Newell strode closer. His sea-green eyes held a gleam; his coal-black hair was wet and slicked back. He was decidedly taller than Maeve's five feet status, and she guessed he was over six feet.

"This isn't the eighteen hundreds, Pierre," Mr. Newell said. "I'm allowed to see my match before our official meeting. I'm sure Mr. and Mrs. ..." He paused.

"Yates, monsieur."

"Right. I'm sure Mr. and Mrs. Yates won't object. Besides, whoever you're hiding isn't my bride. I can take a peek."

"You can take more than a peek, Mr. Newell." Maeve shoved the rigid Pierre aside and held out her hand. "I'm Maeve Doherty."

He seemed stunned for a moment, then delighted, then quickly concealed all reactions. "Very pleased to meet you, Maeve. I'm Edward Newell." He lifted her hand and kissed it. His hand was wet. Drops of water clung to her palm.

He in his wet spandex suit, she in her wrinkled travel clothes, they stood in the marbled lobby of one of the most expensive resorts in the world and warily assessed each other.

At least, Maeve was wary.

She took a quick breath and an even quicker look at Edward. He appeared relaxed, despite his clothes, or lack of clothes. Look up, she scolded herself. Fix your gaze on his face, although her gaze insisted on gravitating downward to his broad, bare chest.

"Hello, Edward." She congratulated herself on being able to speak.

"Now that we've gotten that out of the way," he said. "I recognized you from your photo, although you're much more beautiful in person." His devastating smile held her spellbound. She peered at their hands. They were still connected.

Edward Newell. The name sounded so posh.

His eyes mesmerized her, and she felt a pulse of pure attraction. He could have passed for a swimsuit model. She inhaled a whiff of fresh air and chlorine and affluence. He definitely smelled like a man who enjoyed the good things in life. And if that wasn't enough, she had to concede he was exceedingly handsome.

She could hear Colleen whispering in her ear. *"What if Mr. Right is waiting for you in Corsica?"*

Determined to brazen out their first meet, she turned to

the two men beside them. Pierre's features were well-composed, his gaze was riveted on a point somewhere above her head. The bellhop Nigel stood suspended in midstep, holding onto the luggage cart, apprehension furrowing his brow. Baggage temporarily forgotten, he kept his gaze on the same spot as Pierre.

Evidently impervious to the goings-on around him, Edward kept hold of her hand and used his other one to drape his beach towel more securely around his shoulders. Fit and tanned, his physique was lean and well-toned. Well, except for those shoulders capping off a slim waist. Surely, he must bench-press every day.

"I'm afraid I'm at a disadvantage, Mr. Newell," Maeve said. "I've just arrived and haven't viewed your profile yet."

"There's not much to view, although what I wrote was honest." He studied her with candid interest, still holding onto her hand.

She scraped back her hair with her free hand. Before she'd left Dublin, she'd curled it. Now it hung in loose waves above her shoulders, and she was sure it looked tangled and unmanageable. Why hadn't she taken a second to pull a brush through it? She'd been so anxious to ring her mother and brother, she hadn't focused on anything else.

Aware Edward still scrutinized her, she scrambled for something to say. "I like an honest man," was the best she could come up with.

His lips quirked in a half smile. "And I like an honest woman." Lazily, his gaze dipped, perusing her from the tips of her sensible flats to the top of her hair.

To her chagrin, she felt her cheeks heat.

"So you're from Ireland?"

She lifted her chin. "Aye."

Something flickered in his gaze, and his smile persisted. "You have a lovely Irish brogue, Maeve."

"Thank you." He was a charmer, that was certain. He'd probably dated hundreds of women and planned to cast her onto his list of conquests.

She scanned the lobby. The air hung suspended, and several moneyed tourists openly stared. She imagined Dawson and his crew lurking behind a potted fern and snapping photos of her and Edward.

"I'm from England," Edward continued, "so we don't live far from each other."

"A ninety-minute ferry ride from Dublin across the Irish Sea." She shook her head ruefully. "Of course, you must factor in the additional four-hour train ride from Holyhead in Wales to London."

"Have you ever visited London?"

"Never, although I've known friends who travel to London for soccer matches and concerts."

Edward grinned, his white teeth flashed. "You'll need to update your travel itinerary, Maeve. See the world, live a little."

"Beginning with Corsica, aye?" She drew her hand from his and shot a glance at Pierre. He adjusted his patterned bow tie and patted the yellow square peeking from his breast pocket. "Dinner will be served at eight o'clock this evening."

"We know," Edward and Maeve said at the same time. They shared a chuckle.

"Thank you, Pierre. I'll be there," Maeve agreed.

"Most assuredly, so will I." Very quietly, Edward added, "I'm looking forward to getting to know you better, Maeve."

CHAPTER 4

*M*aeve had followed the bellhop to her second-floor suite.

Although she did not expect that she and Edward would be sharing a room, any hopes that his suite was in another building were quickly dashed. In the Yateses' expectation of a match, they'd booked Maeve and Edward into adjoining rooms separated only by an arched door.

Maeve quickly solved the problem by noisily bolting the door, knowing Edward—who'd followed her and Nigel up the stairs—could hear her key turn in the lock.

What would she say when she called Colleen that night, as she'd promised to do, and Colleen asked what kind of a man Edward Newell was.

"He's fine-looking, I'll give him that," Maeve would answer. "And successful, by the way he carries himself. We met unexpectedly in the lobby. He wore a spandex bathing suit that left little to the imagination and ..."

No, that wouldn't do. Colleen would ask one hundred questions and she'd never allow Maeve to get a good night's rest.

Maeve spent the next few hours unpacking, showering, resting, and finally dressing for dinner.

At seven forty-five, she stared back at herself in the room's full-length mirror. She'd decided to wear her favorite dress, a tie-dyed tank jersey that skimmed her slender figure to mid-calf, accenting her left leg with a side slit.

With a last swipe of rose lip gloss, she slipped on her ankle-strap sandals, grabbed her leopard pouch and walked down the one flight curving staircase. As expected, Pierre was behind his desk, his head bent over a computer.

Briefly, Maeve wondered if he ever slept.

"Miss Doherty." Pierre looked up and immediately became cheerful. "May I show you the terrace? We reserved your table overlooking the harbor and Mr. Newell is waiting for you there."

Here goes, she thought, taking in a deep breath. She'd worked herself into a knot of expectation for what the first dinner might bring with the attractive man she could only envision in a skimpy swimsuit.

Before she'd even unpacked, she had read his dating profile. Actually, she'd read it so much she had it memorized.

Outdoorguy, Age 30

"*Never, never, never give up.*" –*Winston Churchill*

I'm a guy who spends his time outdoors whenever he can get away from work.

It's not often. You see, I'm married ... to my job.

When I do go outside, my dog and I ride my motorcycle as far away from civilization as possible and pitch a tent.

My motto? Enjoy life whenever you can. Every day is a gift.

IN HIS PROFILE PHOTO, he'd obviously just finished playing a pickup football game with friends, judging by the short-sleeved jersey clinging to his muscular shoulders and the beads of sweat on his forehead. A couple of teammates in the background wore wide grins, and they all held up pints of lager. She noticed he didn't.

When Pierre showed her to the terrace, Edward, who had had his cellphone clapped to his ear, immediately disconnected and came to his feet. "Good evening Maeve. You look lovely."

That devastating smile again.

She felt the heat rise to cover her face. "Thank you."

He looked quite fine himself in his elegantly tailored pinstripe suit. His white starched shirt contrasted sharply with his tanned, wind-burned cheeks. His black hair had dried naturally and curled at his nape. Obviously, no fancy hair care products for him.

Pierre bid them a delightful evening as their waiter bore down on them. With a slight bow, he introduced himself as Achille and drew a chair out for her. He had a groomed white mustache and a genial smile.

She paused, taking in the expanse of sea and sky, an occasional whip of a tenacious breeze, the fragrant night air. Realizing Edward and Achille remained standing, waiting for her to sit, she settled into the chair.

Edward sat with his back to the harbor, perhaps out of consideration for her to appreciate the view, perhaps because Achille had directed him to sit there. Regardless, the sight from the wraparound terrace offered fine dining at its best. The Mediterranean night glistened under a bevy of silver stars, and fishing boats swayed side by side amidst million-dollar yachts, gentle waves lapping at the hulls. An occasional seabird swooped, feeding on the Mediterranean's surface.

Achille returned bearing a silver serving tray with a bottle of Champagne in an iced bucket and two fluted glasses. "Because this is your first date, the Yateses insisted you indulge in our finest French Champagne."

Achille set the glasses and equipment on an auxiliary table, drew the cork with a distinctive pop, and carried bottle and glasses to their table.

"Water for me, thanks," Edward said when the waiter began pouring.

"Very good, sir. And you, mademoiselle?"

"I'd love a glass."

The bubbly Champagne flowed, and Achilles waited for her to taste.

She took a sip, and nodded her approval. As Achilles marched back to the kitchen, taking Edward's unused glass, she asked, "You don't drink?"

"Not in eleven years." He shrugged. "I take that back. I imbibed at my parents' twenty-fifth wedding anniversary."

"Congratulations on the longevity of their marriage!"

"They were married thirty years." He paused, and his voice was quiet when he spoke again. "My mother passed away a year later. She's been gone five years now."

Maeve hesitated, trying unsuccessfully to think of something to say, and decided to stick with what was in her heart. "I'm sorry. I'm sure you miss her terribly."

"I do. Thanks." He gave her a thoughtful look. "My siblings and I are all still devastated. She was a courageous woman who fought bravely."

"How did she die?"

"From cancer."

"My sincere condolences." Maeve's thoughts scrambled and with effort she gathered them together. She couldn't face where the discussion might lead—to her brother, his cancer —so she modified the subject. "Otherwise, you don't drink, Edward?"

"Rare occasions."

Achille came back to the table with their menus and recited the catches of the day. "Of the choices, I recommend our Corsican fish. It is prepared unassumingly with olive oil and wrapped in foil. *C'est délicieux!*"

On that recommendation, Maeve ordered the Corsican fish, as well as sautéed potatoes and fresh asparagus. Edward asked for the same.

When the waiter disappeared into the kitchen, Edward lifted his water glass. "I believe a toast is in order. Cheers to us!"

"Aye." With their glasses upraised, they clinked.

She rarely drank, but because she was in a country she'd always fantasized about visiting, because a most attractive man sat across from her, because she needed courage to converse with him intelligently, she told herself it was okay.

"I can't believe I'm here," she declared.

"Neither can I."

She grinned. "It's because of my best friend—"

"It's because of my university friend—" They shared a laugh and clinked glasses again "To friends."

He set down his glass. "So this Perfect Match week wasn't something you agreed to voluntarily?"

"To be honest, no." Somehow, she wanted to tell him more. Perhaps about her brother's illness, her mother's never-ending drama.

No, that wouldn't do. She hardly knew him.

Instead, she drained her glass and clarified, "I'm a friend of Amy Yates."

"Who is she again?"

"Amy and her husband Dawson own the dating agency."

"Right."

"How about you? Why are you here?"

"Hmm?"

He was staring at her so intently she didn't know whether to avoid his gaze or stare back at him. She opted for gazing at the boats in the harbor. "You mentioned your friend," she reminded Edward as Achille appeared to refill her champagne glass.

"Oh, right." There was a long silence before Edward continued. "My friend Bentley decided to play a practical joke and signed me up for this, somewhat of an escapade. When he learned about the joke, my father thought it was an excellent idea. He'd just as soon marry me off to the prettiest woman with two—"

Maeve drew back in her chair and raised her glass to her lips. "Two …?"

"Legs. Two legs." If Edward was trying to look sheepish, the attempt was marred by his boyish grin.

When the meal arrived, she bowed her head and whispered a prayer. Edward didn't participate, although he did bow his head.

More than an hour later, after a lengthy dinner and nonstop conversation, Achille served *fiadone*, a light cheesecake, for dessert. She managed a bite before pushing it to the side. "One word for this cheesecake is a sinful marvel."

"That's two words. Three words if you count the *a*."

She laughed. "I wish I could finish it. It's delicious."

"Do you mind, then?" He waited for her assent before scooping the cheesecake onto his plate.

As he ate, she gazed at the spectacular scene behind him, particularly the way the lights from the town glistened on the harbor's glass-like surface. In her mind's eye, she visualized the panorama at daybreak, sunshine dappling across the boathouses, iron benches set alongside wooden paths leading to the sea, violets and orchids blanketing the flower beds.

The little she'd eaten of dinner had been superb—hot crusty rolls, wafer-thin fish, creamy potatoes, and steaming asparagus sprinkled with parmesan cheese, salt and pepper—all served on porcelain dinnerware, cobalt blue and white, edged in gilded scrollwork. The hectic day of travel, the weather fluctuations from Ireland's dampness to this tropical warmth, so utterly different from her rainy climate, had set her stomach aflutter. Wistfully, she eyed the champagne. She didn't want to waste an entire expensive bottle by drinking only two glasses.

Attributing the delicious warmth flooding her veins to a marvelous evening, she debated indulging in more champagne. However, when Achilles started to refill her glass, she checked him at only a half. Over the rim, she observed Edward. All evening, he'd entertained her with fascinating facts about London's off-the-beaten-path book shops and historical sites. Always soft-spoken, he seemed genuinely interested in the latest Irish scuttlebutt she'd shared, leaning closer, encouraging her to continue whenever there was a lull in their conversation. He exhibited the kind of natural polish she'd observed in the well-heeled clients that frequented Merrimac.

No doubt the other women on the terrace coveted Edward as their date, she thought, for she'd caught more than a few appreciative glances sent his way. Amazingly, this sophisticated and urbane man was with her.

She smiled. He caught her gaze and held it.

And there it was, that tug of attraction.

How? They'd only just met.

As she mulled this over, Edward slanted her a long look. "Quite a day?"

"Aye." She held a hand to her mouth, stifling an unexpected yawn.

"Tired?"

"A little."

"I noticed you didn't eat much, luv." Pointedly, his gaze fell to her empty glass. If he assumed she was feeling a wee bit drunk, he was right.

"I'll make up for my lack of appetite tomorrow," she said. "I love to eat decidedly more than I love to cook."

"I didn't read that bit of information on your profile."

"There's a lot about me you don't know, Edward." She was feeling particularly cheery and unconcerned that she was having trouble focusing. "Do you cook?"

"I prefer takeout, and if I'm forced to host a dinner party, I ring a caterer. I look at the menu online, pick appetizers, a main course, and a dessert, pay the bill, and then I'm done. It doesn't mean I'm lazy," he continued. "It just means I'm inadequate."

She grinned. "I can't imagine you being inadequate in anything."

"There's a lot about me you don't know," he said, parroting her earlier phrase. He pushed back his chair and buttoned his suitcoat. "If you're ready to leave, I'll walk you to your room." He winked. "It's not out of my way."

She laughed again. "Aren't we waiting for someone from the Perfect Match staff to explain what's in store for us this week?"

"Are we?"

"Didn't you read the paperwork?"

He gave a rueful smile. "Clearly not everything."

As if on cue, a pert young woman walked over to their table and introduced herself as Carissa Swanson. She looked to be in her thirties, with a stream of blonde hair. She was a member of the Perfect Match staff. She invited them to sit somewhere else on the terrace that was away from the dining tables.

"I will leave the champagne, mademoiselle?" Achille asked Maeve as he and a busboy discreetly removed plates and silverware. He nodded to Carissa.

"Not a drop more tonight, Achille. Thank you." She placed a hand over the ounce left in her glass, then traced a finger along the cork in the basket. "A cup of hot tea with a spot of sugar sounds good, though."

"Very good, mademoiselle."

Carissa encouraged Edward and Maeve to relax in a cushioned loveseat adjacent to her and urged them to sit close.

She began with a brief description of Perfect Match and the algorithms the company had developed for pairing couples. "We are certain," she went on, "that we've set you two up correctly. For example, you're both workaholics, have never been married, and you both own a dog. Of course, there's more to it than that." She smiled. "But we'll let you two find out those things."

She directed her gaze toward Maeve. "Tomorrow morning at nine o'clock, we'd appreciate footage of you two exploring the island together."

There went her work intentions, Maeve thought. Or maybe she could surreptitiously take notes and photographs of the places they visited to submit to Merrimac Company as potential locations for a new hotel.

"When the sun sets tomorrow night," Carissa continued, "you can frolic in the sea for a swim."

"Frolic?" Edward lifted a dark eyebrow.

"Mr. Yates's word, sir."

"Sorry, but I don't swim." Maeve moved her tea aside. "I don't think I packed a bathing suit ..."

Edward's grin was positively roguish. "If you didn't,

there's a natural bay on the west coast where you can swim without wearing any—"

"I'll buy a swimsuit in the gift shop," she interrupted.

"One piece or two?"

"I'm not certain until I see a style I want to wear."

"I'm partial to string bikinis on women."

Torn between humor and shock, she jibed, "I definitely will *not* keep that in mind."

She blushed easily, an embarrassing giveaway of her emotions, and she felt a tint of heat on her face. With a half giggle, she gaily considered her newest predicament—which swimsuit to purchase. If only life in Ireland could be so uncomplicated.

Carissa left a short while afterward, and Edward and Maeve sat in silence while fragments of conversation from the other diners went on around them. Content with the world, Maeve sighed contentedly and burrowed deeper into the loveseat.

"I didn't know you like dogs," Edward said. Somehow, his arm had ended up around her shoulders as he grinned down at her.

"Doesn't everyone?"

"No. Some people like cats." He brushed a light kiss on her forehead, sending a disturbed flurry of excitement to her pulse. "What's your dog's name?"

"Crinkles. She's a miniature pug."

"A regular-sized pug is small enough to fit in a suitcase. How much does Crinkles weigh?"

"Less than four and a half kilos. Around ten pounds."

"What can a dog that size do besides yap?"

"She's a lapdog. When I get home from work, I'll settle in a comfortable chair by the fireplace with a book in my hand and the drumming of rain on the roof. She cuddles next to me or sits at my feet."

"Do you enjoy reading?"

"Aye."

"Any favorite books? No doubt romance novels, right?"

She hesitated, went for a sip of tea. "My main interest is history, which is the reason why I wanted to come to Corsica."

His smile widened. "Any particular era?"

"The French Revolution, and particularly Napoléon Bonaparte. I admire him as a military commander who led several successful campaigns. Because he was born in Corsica, there's a museum here."

"Remind me to never quarrel with you, if you've read up on Napoléon Bonaparte."

"No worries. I'm very peaceful and will do anything to avoid a conflict." She helped herself to another spoonful of sugar and stirred her tea. "What about your dog? Is she as cute as mine?"

"He, and I'm sure he wouldn't appreciate being pegged as *cute*. He's a black lab and weighs thirty-six kilos." He grinned. "So, eight of your Crinkles. He's a proper dog who rides my motorcycle with me. Plus, we go camping together."

"What's his name?"

"Harley."

"Aye, thus the motorcycle reference in your profile." Maeve nodded and reached for a last sip of tea. Briefly, she savored the lukewarm brew and closed her eyes.

Edward sat so near, the tang of his aftershave scented the brisk evening air. The night was superb, the meal exquisite, and she felt her cares being lifted from her shoulders.

She was so content, she didn't know how much time passed before Edward stood and offered his hand, waiting for her to accept. She couldn't say no, and didn't. As they crossed the lobby, the ever-present Pierre peered up from his computer. "I trust you two had an enchanted evening?" he inquired.

"If you're partial to beautiful Irish women, then mission accomplished." Edward high-signed a salute. "I'd say it was quite marvelous, in fact."

"And you, mademoiselle?"

"Aye. Thank you. Tell Amy and Dawson it was perfect." *More than perfect.*

Hundreds of white votive candles set in glass jars tied with gold ribbons were set on tables throughout the lobby, shooting shadows of light along the marbled floor. The effect was storybook-like, and very, very romantic.

She and Edward climbed the wide, sweeping staircase to the second floor, stopping in front of her door. She leaned against the wall with its patterned wallpaper, her head whirling, and tried closing her eyes. The sensation that she was spinning made her instantly open them again.

She fixated on the soft glowing sconces on the opposite wall and the painting of Corsican orchids. "I never realized I liked champagne so much," she murmured.

He chuckled. "I'll ask your opinion tomorrow morning at nine."

She turned abruptly to bid him good night, overestimated the distance and smacked into his chest. Immediately, his arms encircled her, and he balanced her unsteady footing.

Afterward, when Maeve reviewed what happened next, she upbraided herself for the way she reacted. Rather than staying where she stood with his arms around her, she should have drawn away.

His green-eyed gaze glided to her mouth and his head lowered. As his mouth met hers, his hands skimmed over her hips, drawing her to his muscular build.

She shouldn't have, but her fragile hold on what she should and shouldn't do slipped away while his lips moved boldly over hers. As if it were the most natural thing in the world, she wound her arms around his shoulders and kissed him back.

Dazedly, when she eventually pulled away, it struck her that he'd already released her.

Several seconds passed.

Drawing an unsteady breath, she squinted at him through a haze, distinctly seeing several Edwards standing beneath the portrait of orchids.

More beats.

Finally realizing he was waiting for something, she lifted her eyebrows and said in an overconfident voice, "Do you think I'm going to invite you to my room? Are you hoping that's what happens next?"

"On the contrary, there's an important bit of information about me I wanted to tell you."

"What?"

Please, she thought, *don't let him be married.*

He took a step back and shoved his hands in his pockets. "I don't know how to start, so I'll just say it. Maeve, you're a charming woman."

"Thank you. And you're quite charming yourself."

He nodded but avoided her gaze. "And because of our earlier talk about honesty, I intend to be upfront with you starting now."

She felt herself go still. "Aye?"

Gently, he grasped her forearms. "This week is a bit of a lark for me. As I started to tell you at dinner, my friend Bentley put me up to this and my father seconded the idea. These next few days are a working vacation for me, nothing more. I'm sure you understand, as you're also a workaholic. And for the record, I'm not the marrying type."

Coolly, ungraciously, she shook off his hold. "And you think I am?"

"Look, no matter what happens, we both walk away at the end of the week. No strings, no promises. Agreed?"

"I'm not desperate for love, Edward."

"Good. I don't want you to get hurt."

"By you?" She heard her laugh. It had a cutting edge.

"By any man."

"So this is all a joke, right? This match, this island, me ..."

His eyes flashed. "I wouldn't call it that."

Then what would you call it?

She didn't ask the question out loud as tears of exhaustion and embarrassment sprang to her eyes. The indulgent amusement of the evening had vanished.

He was silent for a moment before he continued. "All I'm saying is we shouldn't spoil a pleasant week with talk of perfect matches or love."

Every muscle in her body quivered. "The last thing I want is a relationship with a man, particularly one who puts his dog at risk."

"What's that supposed to mean?"

She looked away. Heat flushed through her body, which she recognized as mortification for being so impetuous around him. Still, there was no retreating, so she grasped at a flimsy excuse. "I've never seen a dog ride a motorcycle before. What kind of an irresponsible dog owner are you?"

"What? Harley wears goggles and a helmet and rides in a motorcycle carrier, and I'm a most responsible dog owner. Happy now?"

"Nothing you described sounds safe or responsible."

"Take care of your own affairs, Maeve." Edward's gaze narrowed. "Concentrate on what I just said. No strings. Are we in agreement?"

"I haven't the slightest interest in the likes of you."

"That's fine," he said. "But I'm not a betting man, so it's best to clear things up from the starting gate. From what I've gathered, you wouldn't be able to repay such an expensive trip. So let's agree to put on an act for the cameras."

"Actually, I'm a particularly proficient actress."

He shuffled back a step. "Really?"

"Really." She swept out an arm to make her point and knocked the orchid painting to the carpeted floor.

She scrambled to retrieve it, but Edward was faster, hanging the painting back on the wall before she had a chance to sputter another rejoinder.

"Good, it's settled then." He unlocked the door for her and ushered her into her suite. "We'll work together, play together and make this week a resounding success for all of us."

CHAPTER 5

The rap on the door of her suite at precisely nine o'clock in the morning told Maeve it must be Edward. Had she read in his profile that he was punctual, or had she imagined it? He certainly seemed the type ... with his classy ways and ever-pleasant composure.

She'd been frayed the preceding evening and hadn't rung Colleen, although she'd sent a quick text with Edward's name, so at least Colleen had something to go on.

Disheartened by his "honesty," she had tossed in her luxurious king-sized bed and ended up staring at the rotating fan on the high ceiling.

When next she awoke, she saw from her window a golden August moon lighting the sky. She curled onto her side seeking the peacefulness of slumber, but it eluded her. She attributed her restlessness to her pounding headache, which she'd blamed on her champagne overindulgence.

Although she knew it was more.

Edward had informed her in no uncertain terms that he wasn't interested in a romantic relationship.

Which was terrific, because she wasn't interested in one, either.

Although wasn't he the same man who'd seemed mesmerized with her throughout dinner and had kissed her in the hallway outside her suite? She'd seen the desire in his smoky, dark-green gaze. Surely she hadn't imagined it.

Her cheeks burned at how quickly she'd slipped into his arms and returned his kiss. She'd made a brainless fool of herself. And, she vowed, it wouldn't happen again.

She awoke for good at first light, watching the sky transform from blush to peach to vivid orange. She read the book she'd started on the plane, and at half past seven she texted her mother to check on Owen. She had waited because of the one-hour time difference between Ireland and Corsica.

Reassured her brother was doing well, she showered in the spacious Italian-marble shower, and then dressed for the day. She'd pinned her hair in a casual bun, but the sleepless night had left telltale shadows beneath her eyes. However, her jean shorts and a neon-pink tank top made her look fun and young and fit for island exploration.

Again, a knock sounded.

"I'm coming," she called out. She squared her shoulders and dismissed the ruffling in her stomach.

"Corsica discovery, day one," Edward joked as she opened the door. He'd been texting someone. Rapidly, he finished, then stowed the phone into his shorts pocket.

"Sorry. Never-ending business. You know the drill."

No, she didn't. She worked a nine-to-five job at an hourly rate, and wasn't in any position of authority.

He looked exceptionally handsome that morning. He was the sort of man who looked good whether he was dressed for business or leisure. He always looked spot-on. Today, he wore green cargo shorts, a worn navy T-shirt, and black leather mesh shoes. His arms were bare, and a thought zipped through her mind. She wished he hadn't worn a shirt, so she could see his muscled chest.

No, no, no, don't go there. She blamed her speculation on her headache, although despite his dampening comments at the end of the night, his magnetism drew her. She stared at him. Just stared. How could a man be that good-looking?

He strode inside. With a concerned glance at her, he asked how she was feeling.

"Awful." She expelled a shaky sigh. "Most of the night my stomach churned the same as when I arrived, although yesterday I blamed the churning on flight delays and turbulence." She shrugged. "You must have had the same bad weather in London. Did it delay your flight?"

"I flew in from the Continent. I had business to attend to in Nice."

"There's a direct flight from Nice to Corsica?"

"There might be." He shrugged, shifted. "My family owns a private jet."

My family owns a private jet. She massaged her temples and tried to assimilate the information.

"Do you still like champagne?" he asked with a hint of a grin.

"Not nearly as much." She glanced toward the dazzling sunlight filtering through the French doors that led to her balcony and flinched. "My head resembles a soft-boiled egg."

His lips twitched. "I've read it's because of the sulfites in champagne that lots of people have similar reactions, so drink plenty of water today."

She indicated the water bottle she'd placed by her tote bag and attempted a wan smile. "What are sulfites, by the way?"

"No idea." He made a valiant attempt to keep his features straight. "Did you eat any breakfast this morning?"

"Aye, a slice of toast and a bowl of dry cereal."

"Good. I'll order a sports drink for you in the lobby too." He pulled out his phone and quickly texted, she assumed, Pierre.

"Are you an expert on hangovers?" she asked.

"Unfortunately, I am," he said. "Now, ready for a morning of exploration?" He gestured to a daypack thrown over his shoulders.

"Aye." She was wearing sturdy slip-on sneakers and in her jute bag she carried sunscreen, a scarf, and her cellphone for pictures and note taking. She was prepared.

"I went for a run on the beach when I got up and passed Pierre in the lobby before I hit the steam room," Edward said. "As you can guess, he knows our agenda, and it includes les Calanche Cliffs and lunch. Carissa will meet us downstairs." He stared at Maeve's exposed legs, lingering for longer than necessary. "If you stumble and skin your knees, you'll be laid up for the week."

"We're *seeing* the cliffs, not *climbing* the cliffs."

"Right." He took her hands in his. "Did I already tell you that you look lovely today? Despite your fondness for bubbly beverages, you've recovered admirably this morning."

"Thank you. I … no one told me our sightseeing included cliffs and I'm not changing my outfit."

His fingers tightened around hers, his gaze becoming positively seductive. If he tried to kiss her like he did last evening, she'd—

"No doubt," he said, "you didn't thumb through the promotional material, because if you did, you'd have seen our itinerary this morning, which was all about the cliffs," he was saying.

He included a wink that prompted her to laugh. He wasn't going to kiss her, so she needn't fret about how she'd react. She broke from his grip and placed the water bottle in her tote bag. "For the record, I prefer trolling museums. The more ancient the artifacts, the better."

"Ah yes, the Bonaparte museum. So you've mentioned." He rolled his eyes. "Napoléon Bonaparte is on tap for Friday. The Perfect Match specialists planned our activities around the weather report. Friday it's supposed to rain and the museum is our indoor activity."

When they reached the lobby, they were accosted by a bubbly Carissa wearing khaki shorts and a long-sleeved striped shirt.

The ever-present Pierre, although assisting a stout woman obsessed with the breakfast menu, uttered a cheerful "Bonjour" and handed Edward a sports drink "for the mademoiselle."

"We'll take a footpath to the cliffs," Carissa said as she led the way. "The camera crew will meet us there. They'll get shots of you two sitting on the red cliff rocks, cavorting in the sand..."

"Cavorting?" Edward held up a hand. "Don't tell me..."

Carissa nodded. "Dawson's word."

As they trudged the footpath beside roadside vineyards, Carissa spoke nonstop. "After the photo shoot, the waitstaff will provide a picnic lunch for you. Then you're free to spend the afternoon doing whatever you'd like."

A nap, Maeve supposed, but then she remembered she was supposed to be working.

Frothy sea water rolled over the cool, firm sand, and the sea was so blue it was a contest to distinguish where water ended and sky began. Oftentimes both Maeve and Edward paused to take photos with their cellphones, and then Maeve would rapidly type in notes. A spray of salt water often surprised them when a wave crashed close to shore. Boats with billowing white sails navigated the slicing waves in the distant harbor, and the morning sun looked as if it were dusting tiny diamonds across the water.

True to Carissa's word, the camera crew, consisting of a woman and two men, were waiting at the bottom of les Calanche Cliffs when they arrived. Cameras were set up, as well as tripods, light stands and reflectors. A cameraman propped a shade umbrella on a ridge of rocks to protect Maeve's pale complexion from the sun, adding a blanket for her to sit on between takes.

Carissa had even brought along a bouquet of native orange lilies for Maeve to hold while Edward kissed her for a pose.

"Look romantic and affectionate," Carissa directed. "Now can I get a cuddle for another shot? We'll preserve these memories and inspire other couples."

When Carissa announced a wrap at noon, she handed Maeve and Edward clean beach towels. "We're finished for today. You two are so good-looking and natural together. It's as if you've known each other for years and are head-over-heels in love. The chemistry …"

Edward gave Maeve a pat on the shoulder. "That's because Maeve is a professional actress."

"Don't believe a word he says," Maeve ribbed. "He even fakes his British accent."

"And here I was trying to hide my Englishness this whole time." He nudged her elbow. "Well done on discovering my secret!"

After they'd used a nearby restroom, the camera crew and Carissa packed their gear and headed back to the resort.

Four waiters from the hotel delivered a picnic lunch in a wicker hamper. They also set up rainbow-painted canvas chairs, a portable table and a beach umbrella. Efficiently, they served roasted turkey sandwiches on soft pretzel buns, a selection of brie and gouda cheeses, and sliced tomatoes and olives. Dessert included ripe blackberries and squares of dark chocolate. Both Edward and Maeve declined the recommended wine pairings, compliments of Achille, and opted instead for iced tea, bottled water and Maeve's sports drink.

When the last of the luncheon staff departed, Maeve stared at the rising granite rock formations behind them, looking like a pair of gnarled fingers pierced the sky. "My head is still pounding," she told Edward, "so I'm heading back to the resort to work."

"How? It's a long walk back."

"I'll hail a taxi if I get tired. You?"

He scanned the cliff. "I'd like to see where this path leads."

"Don't you need to work too?"

"Yes, but a hike beckons."

She shaded her eyes and peered up. "It's a steep climb."

"But I bet the coastal views are stunning from the top."

"And I'm positive the drop is terrifying if you look straight down." She snatched her tote bag and pivoted toward the footpath. "Happy climbing."

"Maeve? 'The mountains are calling and I must go.'"

She turned. "You couldn't have made that up. Who are you quoting?"

"John Muir. He was from the UK."

"You didn't use his quote on your dating profile."

"I didn't remember it until now." He gestured to a modest sign on the ground. "This path is for beginners and is an easy thirty-minute hike. Don't you want to explore a famous Corsican rock formation with me?"

"Edward, do I look like a person who hikes? The food and shade helped my headache, but I'm bordering on only 50 percent brilliant at best. Besides, you said yourself I'm not dressed for hiking." She turned toward the footpath, again, then turned back to him.

"You're not up for the challenge?" he goaded. "You, a sturdy Irishwoman?"

She wasn't feeling exceptionally sturdy, but she took the bait, especially when he mentioned the lava rocks were two hundred and fifty million years old, and she being a history buff and all ….

He'd neglected to mention that although there were no words to describe the stunning natural landscape when they reached the top, the hike would leave her breathless. The trail led sharply through the woods. Loose stones were everywhere, and she lost her footing several times on the dangerous, heart-stopping corners.

He frequently steadied her, much as he had the night before, with one arm around her shoulders. Many times she questioned aloud why she'd agreed to go with him; and he smiled, calm and patient, and offered to carry her tote bag. When she told him he didn't need to hover beside her every minute, he went ahead, although he glanced behind often. Moreover, he took numerous breaks, pausing to snap photos of the scenery until she caught up.

An hour later, she wiped her perspiring face and pushed strands of hair from her forehead, as most of her hairpins had fallen to the ground.

So much for a casual bun. So much for a thirty-minute hike.

He yanked a thin jacket from his day bag and laid it down for them to sit on. They rested on a notched rock with a marvelous view of the entire Calanche area. The lights and shadows of the cliffs, the colors, fluctuated with the angle of the sun, and the rough and wild coastline spread far and unknown beneath them. Maeve admired the panorama as the howl of the ocean whistled between the rocks and a light mist of brine settled on her cheeks.

"Corsica is magnificent, isn't it?" she mused.

"Extraordinary." He gestured at the wind-eroded rocks. "How does it feel to be a mountaineer?"

"Exhilarating and exhausting. You were right though. The view is worth it."

He drew two bottles of water from his bag and offered her one.

"What do you do for a living?" he asked when she'd taken a swig of water and rested against the rocks.

From the tangled underbrush, she plucked a fistful of rosemary and sniffed the mint-like aroma. "I work for a hotel firm, the Merrimac Company. I'm one of the purchasing agents."

"What are you in charge of buying?"

"Mostly seating and lighting. I compare prices and quality. We're small, and I pride myself on contracting the lowest bids for everything I order."

"A good purchasing agent can make or break the profits of a hotel."

"I'd like to work up to a position in management. Merrimac is based in Ireland. Have you heard of it?"

He drained his water bottle and jammed it into his bag. "England and Ireland are separated by a brief ferry ride, if you recall," he teased.

"If it's pouring rain, then the trip wouldn't be quite as brief, I suppose." She chuckled and took another sip of water. "What about you? What do you do for a living?"

"I own a hotel resort firm, Penelope and Edward International. Or rather, my father owns the company and I'm vice president."

She touched a hand to her chest and silenced her gasp.

Penelope and Edward International? The single most distinguished hotel conglomerate in the world, boasting resorts in America, Europe and Asia.

She gazed at a rock formation resembling a staircase so

she wouldn't gaze in shock at him. "You actually own Penelope and Edward?"

"My family does, although I'm at the helm now, being the oldest son. Old-fashioned values and all that. My father is impatient to retire."

At her quizzical look he went on. "Penelope was my mother's name. She and my father established their first resort hotel thirty years ago. They learned a lot, struggled a lot and invested judiciously. My father's name is Edward."

"And you're Edward the second?"

That explained it, she thought. *His refinement, his utterly sophisticated manner, his private jet.*

He chuckled. "You make me sound like royalty which I can confirm I'm not."

"So you're not Lord Edward, and I can most assuredly verify I'm not Lady Maeve."

Where was this leading? she wondered, setting her water bottle down. He *owned* one of the most luxurious hotel resort chains in the world. She *worked* at a hotel as an employee in the marketing department. Big difference.

Breaking the silence, he pointed outward toward an inlet. "I'll explore that area tomorrow, along with the lengthy stretch of beach. Penelope and Edward is weighing options for another resort, which is why this is a working holiday for me."

"Coincidentally, my company is seeking a place to expand as well. They prefer a site that has an existing property, thus *my* working holiday."

Before she could react, he brought her hands to his lips and kissed her palms. "Maybe the Perfect Match specialists knew what they were doing after all. We have so much in common."

The light from the afternoon sun enhanced the laugh lines around his sensual mouth, and she was powerless to tear her gaze away from his persuasive green eyes. A gust kicked up, blowing her remaining hairpins onto the rocks and tossing her shoulder-length hair in all directions. Distractedly, she pulled her hands from his grip and reached for the crinkly scarf she'd packed inside her tote bag. She twisted the scarf's edges, folded it around her hair, and double knotted it.

"Wouldn't you agree, Maeve? We get along so well." He checked her busy hands. "We're never at a lack for words. Perhaps we are made for each other."

"You're joking, right? Not for one minute are we alike. First, you're ignoring the fact I'm far from wealthy by your lofty standards, and second—"

"We're both here, aren't we?" His voice was quiet, seductive.

"Aye, for a week. You're either very fluthered or—"

"I don't drink, remember?"

She primly folded her hands on her lap. "I forgot you're a holy joe."

"I'm sensible."

"After your elegant speech last night," she said, "we both know this conversation isn't a good idea. Next time I'll throw more than a wall hanging at you if you try to kiss me."

"And here I assumed you were trying to elbow that painting off the wall just to test Newton's theory of gravity."

Slowly, he drew her to him.

She started to pull back, but his arms tightened around her. At the initial contact of his lips on hers, she froze. He continued, biding his time, his fingers caressing her cheeks, smoothing and shaping, his mouth bold yet tender.

"Edward, I won't be able to forgive you this time," she murmured against his lips.

"I'll take my chances," he whispered.

The taste of his mouth on hers, the hard, male strength of

his body, brought a humming to her veins. She tried to keep her hands in her lap, but they slid around his neck of their own accord. The more boundless the kiss, the more yielding she became.

When the kiss ended, she rested her face against his chest. Disoriented, she struggled to analyze her emotions. Although angry at him, she was angrier at herself. She'd vowed she wouldn't become another of his conquests, a woman he had fun with for a week and then discarded. Nonetheless, his charm disarmed her at every corner.

On a sultry August day in Corsica, even the breeze was hot; and the sharp taste of the salty ocean air, even as high up as they were, reminded her of the waves pounding below them.

"Are you ready to leave?" he asked.

After that kiss? She glanced at him, but he'd set his features on neutral. Oh, if only her emotions weren't such an open book.

"We'll go down the same path, as we're familiar with the terrain," he continued, peering at his expensive watch, the dial illuminated. "It's three in the afternoon, and we'll pace ourselves since the grade is so steep. I have responsibilities to attend to before dinner, but I've got five hours to get everything accomplished."

"I have work too, remember?"

"As I pointed out, we're both workaholics." With that, he grabbed her water bottle, tightened the cap and added it to his day bag. He offered his hand and brought her to her feet, then tied his jacket around his waist. "Another reason we should head down is because …"

"Dinner is at eight," they said together, and laughed.

A low-hanging mist hampered their progress down the cliff. They stopped often, and had to use their hands to keep from sliding downhill.

"Look ahead, stay centered," Edward instructed. "Take small steps. We're nearing the bottom."

"It's steep and slippery in this one patch." She went to grab a slender tree branch and lost her balance. The scenery tilted and blurred. Her muscles knotted.

She was falling and there was no way to stop it.

She screamed, groping blindly. Stone scraped her bare arms and legs. Soon she'd be plunging through empty air.

"Maeve!"

Scrambling for something to hold onto, she caught sight of Edward, his face ashen as he tore downhill and caught her. With her in his arms, he lost his footing, and they landed together on the uneven ground.

They both saw it. The odd twist of his ankle as he rolled to the side.

Immediately, he stood up and limped two steps.

He looked pale. She righted herself and gripped his hand. His pulse was unsteady.

"I think I sprained it." His gaze flitted from his ankle to the path. "I don't think I can walk."

"I'll go for someone. There must be a physician on this island."

He swayed as she steered him to a sheer vertical rock wall. He leaned into her, so much so that she was barely able to support his solid body. Inch by inch she assisted him as he braced a hand behind himself and sat. An oath escaped him.

"I'll ring for help." She snatched her cellphone from her tote bag and punched in the resort's phone number.

Oh no. No service in this remote area.

How was she going to assist a man twice her size down a cliff when he'd twisted his ankle?

She flopped down beside him and ran a shaking hand through her hair.

"Maeve, are you all right?" He gritted his teeth as he

leaned forward and brushed her knee where blood streamed from a gash.

"Me? Aye, of course. I'm a sturdy Irishwoman, remember? You're the worry." She pulled the scarf off her hair and patted her knee with it. Then she removed the shoe and sock off Edward's injured foot, untied his jacket from his waist and used it to wrap his ankle. "Just rest for now," she said calmly, much more calmly than she felt. "There are plenty of hours before dark."

She set his day bag on the ground. His ankle was swollen and obviously tender to the touch judging by the way he tightened his fingers around his bag and avoided her gaze.

Carefully, she settled his foot onto her lap. He winced.

"I'll head to the restroom area below," she said. "It's not far. There should be cellphone service there and I'll ring for help."

He grimaced and sat stiffly against the rock. "You're a good caregiver, Maeve."

"Aye, it's what I do best." She considered his handsome face. This close, she could see the flecks of gold in his green eyes, his long, soft lashes. "Does your ankle hurt much?"

"Yes." He managed a smile. "If I were a drinking man, I'd go for a glass of last night's champagne about now."

"Believe me." She gave a doleful laugh and carefully elevated his foot on his day bag. "You'd be sorry tomorrow."

"Maeve." He grasped her fingers as she stood. "Can I admit I don't want you to leave me?"

She saw the effort it took for him to ask the question, his steely self-control exposed.

"You can admit whatever you'd like." She pressed her hand against his cheek, an act of comfort. "I won't be gone long, I promise."

And with that guarantee, she began her descent.

CHAPTER 6

*M*aeve was more than an exceptional caregiver, Edward decided the following morning as he finished a business negotiation with his sister. She was an angel.

After she'd gotten him settled against the rock wall, she'd hurried down the cliff and then came back within a few minutes. Winded, she'd apparently run the entire course. She had been able to use her cellphone at the base and had called Pierre, who had immediately contacted the nearest hospital.

Thirty minutes later, medical aid arrived. By stretcher, the medics carried Edward to the main road where an ambulance idled, waiting to transport him to an accident and emergency center.

Maeve remained with him in the rear of the ambulance, lightly stroking his hair, telling him everything would be all right in a voice clogged with tears, which betrayed her assurances. She'd been more worried about him than he was, unable to hide the concern in her eyes, and his heart had filled with appreciation.

When they'd reached the center, Dr. Dubois, a portly man

in his fifties, had assessed Edward's range of foot motion. After X-rays and because Edward was able to walk without any aids, the doctor had determined no bones were broken.

"I recommend crutches, and I won't need to see you again unless your ankle isn't healing properly." Dr. Dubois's gaze shot to Maeve. "In the interim, your lovely nurse will help you get around."

"Oui, she's a tremendous support," Edward agreed.

With that pronouncement, every person in the examining room turned to look at Maeve.

She'd laughed a denial, then angled her head to the side to avert their stares. A flattering pink bloomed on her cheeks, resembling an early-summer rose, utterly charming against her creamy skin.

Through his discomfort, her blush had coaxed a grin from him.

Now it was a day later, and nearly noon.

Edward settled into the cushioned chair on his suite's balcony. Despite his original doubts about this trip, the days were passing surprisingly fast.

Maeve stood in his efficiency kitchen, cobbling together a sandwich for his lunch—thinly sliced turkey, cheddar cheese, mustard and a side of crisps. Although the resort had offered to cater their meal, she'd instead insisted the staff provide ingredients so she could prepare the sandwiches herself.

She pleated white linen napkins, then creased the napkins into a three-way pocket and slipped the utensils inside.

"Did you hear what I said, Edward?" she called.

"Hmm?" He'd been staring at her. She looked so provocative in cut-off jean shorts, bare feet and one of his worn chambray shirts, which she'd tucked into her shorts. She'd spilled orange juice on her blouse when preparing him breakfast, and although she'd unlocked the adjoining door to her suite, she hadn't returned to change after he'd offered one of his shirts.

She tilted her head to look at him. "I said, do you want a cup of coffee with your sandwich?"

"I drank my quota for the day, thanks." Along with eating enough tangy grapefruit that morning to cure the most jaundiced sailor while Maeve had itemized the benefits of vitamin C.

At first, the pain in his ankle had dominated Edward's attention. Now the pain rested quietly in the background, thanks to compression dressing, ibuprofen and Maeve's tender care.

After carefully showering, he'd thrown on a pair of fleece shorts and a Snoopy T-shirt. Now he sighed and stretched, comfortable and content.

"Don't forget," Maeve said, "that the doctor advised the twenty/twenty rule. Ice on your ankle for twenty minutes, then twenty minutes off. We don't want you to get frostbite."

"Oui, mademoiselle," he teased.

"I've always wanted to learn how to speak French." Finished with plating his sandwich and a salad for herself, she poured a glass of cold tea for him and mineral water for herself.

"Because my hotels are international," he said, "I'm fluent in the French language. I can teach you if you're interested."

She smiled over her shoulder at him and set the food and drinks on a tray. "I'd like that."

The way her dark eyes shone a deep, sincere brown, the way she carried herself—proud and graceful—sparked something inside him. He didn't know what to call it, couldn't give it a name, this strange feeling in his gut each time he looked at her.

Walk off at the end of the week, he reminded himself. *No emotional hassles were the best approach to relationships with women.*

It had suited him well in the past. The women he dated knew the score. No tension, no promise of commitment, only a brief physical connection.

Yet with Maeve, already their relationship spun with warm-heartedness and a joggle of attraction he couldn't deny. He recalled the way her face had lit up when she'd described her dog, her Irish flat, her love of history. He liked a woman with a craving for life. Dating a woman like Maeve, he'd never be bored.

When a knock sounded on the door, Edward called for the person to come in. A ramrod-straight Pierre stood in the doorway. When he spotted Edward sitting on the balcony, his foot elevated, his pained expression affirmed that Edward's ankle sprain had somehow been his fault. "Mr. Newell, I am so sorry about your accident," he apologized for what had to be the six thousandth time. "I telephoned Mr. and Mrs. Yates and they are very concerned."

With a brief nod at Pierre, Edward puffed out a breath, wracking his brain for a way to get rid of the man.

"Must be a busy day for you, Pierre," he said. "I overheard a huge number of people from a cruise ship are checking in around noon."

The concierge gawked at his watch, and his eyes widened. "Oui, monsieur. I almost forgot."

"Well then, au revoir." Edward glanced at Maeve and winked. "That means goodbye in French."

She smirked. "Merci."

Pierre's gaze swung to her. "A staff member will check on Monsieur Newell later. May I remind you both that dinner is at eight o'clock, and Achille is serving roasted boar and zucchini beignets. Does that suit, mademoiselle?"

"We're brilliant here, Pierre," she said. "And I'm sure

dinner tonight on the terrace will be magnificent." Maeve continued to slice up strawberries and blackberries, combining scoops of them into a crystal bowl. "Everything is lovely, really. You should go."

A frown creasing his normally good-natured expression, Pierre demonstrated a perfect bow and quit the room.

Maeve carried the luncheon tray onto the balcony. She nodded at his cellphone, which had been attached to his ear for nearly three straight hours. "Edward, I think you should slow down your activities this afternoon."

"You mean I overdid it with my walk from the couch to out here this morning?"

"You should have used your crutches." She set the tray on the wrought iron table. "Crutches aren't doing you any good propped against the couch."

"I don't need them."

"Because you leaned on me whenever you got up and moved anywhere." With that laughing reminder, she went into his suite for a bucket of ice and a thin towel. Reappearing, she enfolded the ice in the towel, then gently wrapped the towel around his elevated ankle.

"The swelling is better," she said. "You're a good and proper patient and do what you're told."

"And you're the first person who's ever claimed that about me, at least the *do what you're told* part."

Her smile dazzled him, and he could think of nothing he would rather do than kiss the mischievousness from her face. Instead, he ran his finger around the rim of his iced tea glass. "Thanks to you I'm feeling better."

"Thanks to Dr. Dubois." She settled onto the chair across from him and peered at the killer-view vista of sea and sky and cliffs.

Edward's gaze shifted to her. "I realize employment calls,

and yet you're devoting every spare minute to me. Thank you."

"You're very welcome." She withdrew her fork from the folded napkin, set her napkin on her lap, and said a prayer. Then she poked at the lettuce on her plate. "You have work too."

"Which I attended to this morning and I'm taking the rest of the day off. But you have a boss to answer to."

"Right. Because you're the vice-president and I'm a mere worker bee."

True, he thought, understanding what else she didn't say. The enormous wealth gap between them that she had pointed out the day before. She was dressed in the most casual of clothes, and she'd secured her dark hair with an elastic band in a spur-of-the-moment bun at the top of her head. She certainly didn't have the means to purchase expensive clothes or jewelry like Davinia, the raven-haired heiress he'd been dating on and off for a couple years, yet no one looked as radiantly striking as Maeve, his compassionate caregiver with the gentle mannerisms and dainty, endearing profile.

He took a bite of his sandwich, briefly closed his eyes and sighed. "This is delicious."

"Thanks, I'm an expert at sandwich preparation because I've made hundreds in my lifetime."

He laughed. "Sandwiches for yourself?"

"Aye, and my brother Owen. He's twenty, in case you're interested."

"I'm interested in anything that has to do with you. Is he attending university?"

"He was, but he dropped out. He needs a lot of care."

Edward caught the word *care*. Instantly attentive, he sat straighter. "Why? Is he ill?"

Her earlier smile faded. "He has cancer. Thankfully, he's in remission."

Memories rushed to the fore of his mother's battle with cancer. It had been a life changer as his family adjusted to the new situation, the daily activities, the skilled medical team eventually brought into his parents' home. Even his stalwart father had, at times, been just as anxious and felt just as helpless as his sons.

"I'm sorry." Edward stayed silent for a moment. "I know firsthand how scared you and your mother must be."

"Aye." Maeve laid down her fork. Sadness lived on the edges of her nod. "When you spoke of your mother's passing the other evening at dinner, I considered telling you, but didn't want to burden you with my troubles. Part of my hesitation was selfishness, I suppose, for speaking of Owen's illness makes me sad."

He pondered this before treating himself to another bite of sandwich. "And your mother? How is she handling your brother's illness?"

"My mother … Well, she has many interests besides Owen, especially since my father walked out on us a few years ago."

Setting his sandwich down, Edward scooped up a handful of crisps. "Somehow I sense you're the strong one in the family."

She waved a dismissive hand. "Truly, you're giving me credit I don't deserve. Anyone would do the same and take care of the ones they love." She stabbed more lettuce with her fork. "I spoke with my mother last night, as a matter of fact, and she mentioned things are brilliant. You see, Owen moved in with her while I took this holiday. She's enjoying his company so much she suggested he live with her permanently until he lands a job and secures his own flat. It'll be good for them both to grow closer." She sighed. "Still, I'll miss not seeing him on my couch every evening."

Typical Maeve, Edward thought. Concerned about everyone except herself, wearing her sentiments on her sleeve, forever fair and honest. Deep in his chest, a heartrending affection blossomed, a protectiveness to keep her safe from sadness and hardships, and the emotions both bewildered and disquieted him. He chewed a crisp, swallowed, then picked up his iced tea and drank half the glass.

For the first time, he considered that he wouldn't be seeing Maeve again after this week. How could he return to London in a few days with only the remembrance of her lilting laugh, her pleasant ways, her kind compassion? With the afternoon sun illuminating her face, she looked so delicate, so gorgeous, she seemed almost ethereal.

As he set his iced tea glass down, she gave him a curious look. "You said the other night that you don't drink."

"Not a drop."

"May I ask why?" She waited. The silence between them interrupted solely by the sound of splashing waves below them.

He sat back in his chair. "When I attended university, one of my classmates was seriously injured in a car accident. He'd been drinking heavily. We all had been. He should never have gotten behind the wheel. Then, in a blink"—Edward snapped his fingers—"his car ran off the highway. Now he's paralyzed from the waist down. Fortunately, no one else was hurt."

"Oh my." She held a hand to her heart. "I'll say a prayer for him."

Edward pushed out a sigh. "I make it a point to visit him whenever I can, as he lives near London." He disposed of the towel, now dripping wet from melted ice, that she'd wrapped around his ankle. He stretched out his long legs and glanced at her. She was frowning. "The twenty/twenty rule," he reminded her. "It has to be twenty minutes from now."

"So," he went on, steering the conversation in a different direction to lighten the somber moods of cancer and drunken car accidents, "who's watching Crinkles this week?"

"My mother. And your motorcycle-riding dog?"

"One of my brothers, Justin, keeps him, and you'll be relieved to know Justin doesn't ride a motorcycle." He leaned across the table and tipped up her chin. "So no worries."

Their gazes locked. He kept his hand on her chin.

Her dark eyes flashed. "Edward, remember my warning."

"What warning?"

"You know perfectly well."

He did, but he wouldn't be admitting it.

"Let's talk about your siblings." She shoved up the sleeves of his shirt and sat back. "What are their ages?"

"Twenty-eight, twenty-six, and twenty-four. And you know my age from my profile."

"Aye. You recently turned thirty. And their names?"

"Bryan, Justin and Karen. Bryan's twenty-six and Karen is twenty-four. She's very hands-on and business oriented, and helps me quite a bit with the company, but she's also unhappily married. Justin is in the middle. He was married for five years and is recovering from a bitter divorce that almost destroyed him. I learned something from Karen and Justin."

"Let me guess. You vowed never to marry."

"Guys like me are better off single. My parents worked nonstop to develop our business and I intend to continue the expansion. I'm married to my work."

"As well you should be, with all you own." She set her napkin on the table and glanced at her watch. "Well, it's more than time for me to leave. Thanks for a brilliant lunch."

"You've barely eaten."

"I've consumed more these past couple days than I

normally eat in a month. For now, I should head back to my suite and input a couple hours' worth of reports before dinner. I can't afford to lose my job. Owen's medical bills are staggering. He has insurance, though it's not enough. Fortunately, I was able to assure my manager, Mrs. McShea, that I'd be effective this week. So far, I haven't managed to get an ounce of work done and don't even know if my computer works."

Right away, Edward felt remorseful. He was keeping her from her job and monopolizing her. His injury didn't require her to wait on him because the efficient hotel personnel were more than delighted to accommodate his requests. He simply wanted her to stay because he liked being around her.

She came to her feet and began stacking plates. "What about your work? After all those phone calls this morning, I'm thinking you've probably got paperwork to catch up on."

What work? What paperwork?

He stared out at the ocean, the sheer vastness that stretched to the horizon, the waves taking their cue from a sea breeze. What was truly important? Work? Family? Marriage and children as his father claimed?

He'd made a fortune following his father's lead, inputting his own grit and perseverance, along with solid investments. What did he have to show for it? Well, he'd purchased a palatial estate in Surrey in a million-dollar suburb outside London. The six-bedroom home was perched on the banks of a river and surrounded by acres of green space. He rattled around in the hollow house and seldom entertained. He was too busy working.

A golf course was nearby, but he'd never golfed in his life. He preferred a more energetic sport like soccer. To him, golf was a mental game and not physical enough.

In truth, he was too busy … working.

Seconds ticked by. He noted Maeve watching him.

"My job is challenging," he finally said.

Her eyes widened in mock surprise. "Really?" She broke into a smile. "How do you manage such a huge conglomerate of resort hotels?"

"We employ an exceptional staff. Several smaller chains fall under the Penelope and Edward International umbrella as well, so not every hotel is a large resort. In addition, more than half are franchised."

His cell phone buzzed with a text message. He glanced at it and smiled. "Tomorrow we're going deep sea fishing."

She lifted a delicate eyebrow. "Are we now, knowing I can't swim?"

He grinned. "Our itinerary—"

"What about the Bonaparte Museum, the only tourist site on *my* wish list and the main reason I wanted to come to Corsica?"

He put on an expression of horror. "A *museum*? And here I thought you came here for me."

"If you recall, I didn't even know who you were."

Employing his most charming grin, he said, "Bonaparte Museum is on our schedule for Friday when it rains, remember? On Thursday, I'm interested in exploring the stretch of beach I pointed out to you. Are you okay with that? I'm sure Pierre can provide transportation."

"Aye. Although I'm warning you, I'll be sending a report to my boss too, especially if there's an existing hotel on site." She put on a haughty expression. "And I'll be getting the most excellent prices on the lighting and seating because I drive a hard bargain."

He nodded in acknowledgment of her superiority. "Which companies do you acquire from?"

"Mostly J and J Hospitality."

"An excellent supplier."

She laughed. "So, on Thursday we may be at war over a stretch of beach.

"I'll never be at war with you, Maeve," he said in a tone that brooked no argument. "And if I ever am, with your knowledge of battle history, you'd win."

"Your resources are stronger than mine. Wealth, power—"

"That means little when it comes to you." He hobbled to his feet, grabbed the plates from her hands and set them on the table. "Stay a while longer." He sat down again. "It's quiet and private here."

"Being alone with you isn't necessarily a good thing for me."

"Why not?" He captured her wrists. When she didn't pull away, he drew her down on his lap. Her scent was floral with a hint of citrus, adrift on the warm summer breeze.

"All this is make-believe, Edward, not real life. You and I both know where it ends."

For a long while, he stared at her. "I'm sorry you feel that way. These past few days have been some of the most enjoyable of my life. And I think you're the prettiest, most captivating woman I've ever met."

Silently, she scanned every inch of his face. "You must say that to every female."

"No, just one Irish lady who has me wanting to spend every minute with her." He traced his fingers along her high cheekbones. "When I'm with you, I forget about conglomerates and franchises and high-pressure meetings. You have a sense of serenity about you, Maeve."

She looked down, rerolling one of the sleeves of his chambray shirt. "And now, after all this flattery, you're waiting for an excuse to kiss me, I suppose."

"I don't need an excuse." He gathered her closer. "Although truer words have never been spoken."

Her gaze lifted to his, silently enticing.

It was all the encouragement he needed.

His mouth slanted over hers as he kissed her greedily. She circled her arms around his neck and kissed him back. For an eternity, their lips merged as she molded herself to him. Strands of hair fell from her loose bun, and the fine dark strands brushed against his cheek.

He deepened the kiss, cradling her face, whispering how exquisitely she fit into his arms. When his lips left hers, she drew a ragged breath and snuggled against him.

They stayed that way for an endless moment, and when she began to stir, he tightened his arms around her. "Wait another moment, luv."

The thought that they could stay like this forever, in this halcyon place, her body fitted so perfectly to his, filled him with a joyful spirit, one so happy, he hardly recognized himself.

Somewhere close by, a turtle dove cooed on a bough.

He looked out again at the ocean and the sandy shore, the smudges of royal-blue sky on the horizon. He imagined the waves tumbling over seashells and snatching them back into the ocean.

"Edward."

Her voice drew his gaze back to her. She was looking up at him, desire smoldering in her brown eyes.

"Yes?"

"I should leave. I have my job."

"If you insist on staring up at me with that expression ..." His lips strayed to hers. "I guarantee you won't be getting a morsel of work done today."

She twisted from his arms and leapt to her feet. "Shall we put more ice on your ankle?"

With that, she boosted him to the living room couch. While he dried his foot with a spare towel, she made another ice compress and then wrapped it around his ankle. He dragged a sock over it to hold it in place.

With no more warning than a knock on the door and a "Anybody home?" Carissa pranced into Edward's suite holding the hallway orchid portrait. "This fell off the wall. I'll let Pierre know." She gestured to the cameraman who'd stepped in behind her. "I'm hoping for a brief shot of you two today since we missed last evening's photo shoot on the beach."

"Carissa, I'm a fright." Maeve ran her fingers through her hair, dislodging the elastic that held it in its untidy bun. "Tell Mr. and Mrs. Yates to wait until tomorrow for better promotional material."

Fright was not the word Edward would use to describe Maeve. Her silky waves of hair teased her shoulders. Her lips, he noted, were the color of an enticing plum wine, and she looked like a woman who had just been thoroughly kissed.

"Nonsense, Maeve," Carissa said, "you're always gorgeous. Just stand together near the couch. And Edward—" Carissa clucked at his jersey shorts, then brushed crumbs from the neckline of his T-shirt. "You'll have to do. Sorry about your ankle calamity, by the way."

"I'm recovering nicely." He grinned as Maeve helped him stand.

Carissa regarded them intently, then frowned. With practiced actions, she snagged the orange lilies from the crystal vase set on the coffee table. "Maeve, hold these, and Edward, brace yourself on your crutches or you'll knock Maeve over."

Carissa stepped back, reassessed, still frowned. "Let's prop the orchid painting on the shelf behind you for color interest."

The cameraman shot multiple images until Carissa, apparently satisfied, pivoted on her ruby-red pumps, and headed for the door. "Tomorrow is deep-sea fishing," she reminded them. "And tonight, dinner is at ..."

"Eight o'clock," they all chimed.

Still chuckling as the door closed behind Carissa and the cameraman, Edward turned to Maeve. Her cheeks were flushed with high color, her laughter filling the air with goodness and pure joy. More and more, everything about the tempo of their days together—the sun-drenched island, his attraction to her, spending every waking minute with such an incredible woman—felt absolutely and utterly spot-on.

CHAPTER 7

*S*porting a wide-brimmed straw hat, Maeve took one last glimpse at her reflection before answering Edward's nine o'clock morning rap on her suite's door.

The night before, dinner had been expertly prepared, and she'd eaten her way through the entire meal, having discovered a love for zucchini beignets and all things French.

It seemed half the island of Corsica had dined on the terrace along with them, and Edward had reminded her that a cruise ship carrying hundreds of passengers had arrived that day. And, he'd recapped as he'd stabbed a slice of wild boar, La Bonaparte Resort was a three star Michelin resort—the highest rating—and dining there was a "must stop" in all the guidebooks when visiting Corsica.

She'd rung her mother after breakfast and been reassured her brother was fine, and then Maeve finally called Colleen. As expected, Colleen peppered their conversation with complaints about Ireland's nonstop rain, and then had demanded every detail concerning Edward and his ankle sprain, which Maeve had texted her about. Maeve acknowledged she was enjoying an altogether marvelous week and hadn't logged onto her computer once. Therefore, she hadn't produced a smidgen of work.

How could she when thoughts of romance and happiness consumed her?

Dare she dream?

Love consumed her.

"How's Edward?" Colleen asked, obviously settling in for an interrogation. "Tell me everything."

"Well, he's drop-dead handsome and kind and charming …"

"When you sent your text with his name the other day, I did some probing on the internet. Are you aware he's a billionaire and one of the wealthiest men in the world? And he's a member of the three-comma club."

"What's that?'

"Do the math. It's his yearly income, whereas ours has no comma." Colleen chortled. "His family owns Penelope and Edward International. You know, that hotel chain manages over one thousand resorts and rents two hundred thousand rooms a year."

"He certainly doesn't flaunt his wealth. He's funny and down-to-earth and smart. And we always eat together for dinner. In fact, yesterday we had lunch in his suite."

"Go on."

"Even though I'm seeing him often, we never run out of things to talk about." Maeve rubbed a hand across her temple. "Colleen, it's beautiful here, and he's so attentive and—"

"You sound like you're already half in love with him."

"I'm simply a princess in a fairy-tale. He's my prince, and relies on me to get around."

Truth nudged. She knew he was using his ankle as an excuse to be near her, but she certainly didn't mind.

"You're a caregiver, Maeve, but Edward isn't your

brother. He's a rich playboy, if the reports in the tabloids are true. Sorry to burst your bubble, princess, but I don't want you to get hurt again. Remember your last boyfriend?"

"It's different this time. Edward's a good man and the complete opposite of Finbar."

"And you're a good woman. Enjoy yourself while you're there, just keep a clear head."

"I will." With a nod into the phone, Maeve clicked off.

She'd slept deeply and easily the night before, burrowing into the decadently thick covers and dreaming of a tall handsome man with hair the color of ebony and eyes as green as shamrocks. She wanted to deny the magnetism, like a bolt fastening her to him, as if they'd always been together. As if … She sighed.

Still, she couldn't ignore Colleen's warning. Hinging any hopes of a future with Edward, of love and commitment, well, the mere personification of the idea was meant to cause her heartache and pain. The outcome was as plain as a dark, drizzly Irish winter.

She opened her door and Edward walked gingerly into her suite. He wasn't using his crutches, again, and was careful not to put his full weight on his hurt ankle. He wished her good morning in French and then peered at her. "Anything the matter?"

"No, of course not." She swallowed hard against the lump in her throat.

Who were dreams for, she asked herself, all those fabulous Cinderella stories? The young and the foolish. Certainly not for her. Love happened to other people.

"Good," he said. "You're a treat to look at, as pretty as a gourmet candy."

"A compliment, aye?"

"Absolutely."

"I bring out the kid in you?"

"And the adult." He drew her into his arms, cuddling her for a long kiss. "Ready for Corsica Adventure Day Three?"

When she stepped back from his embrace, he scanned her tasseled swimsuit coverup, which featured a glimpse of her bare shoulders. "I'm glad you were able to pick up something pretty at the gift shop."

"I ducked into the gift shop after dinner last night, before the shop closed."

He quirked a dark eyebrow. "Is your swimsuit one piece or two?"

"You're really asking me that question?" She jabbed a playful fist at his forearm. "I'll surprise you."

"Excellent. I have a surprise for you tonight too."

"What is it?"

He grinned. "If I tell you, it would spoil the surprise."

He wore washed-out board trunks, and she was grateful he hadn't worn his tiny spandex swimsuit, for she wouldn't have known where else to look but at his perfectly-toned abs.

Mirrored aviator sunglasses were hooked onto the front of his Linus and Lucy T-shirt.

"Evidently you're partial to the Peanuts comic strip?" she noted.

"I read the daily comics, even now when they're in reruns. Since you're such a history buff, you'll be interested in this. Did you know Peanuts ran from the year 1950 to 2000, and it's been suggested it's the longest running story ever told?"

"Very interesting." She peered down at his ankle. On his feet he wore a pair of slide sandals stamped with a designer logo. "Umm, where are your crutches?"

"Don't need them, as long as I have someone to lean on."

"How's your ankle?"

"Better. Dr. Dubois said everyone heals differently. I'm apparently a fast healer."

She sighed. "And men always hear what they want and

dismiss the rest. If you recall, Dr. Dubois also said you could easily injure your ankle again, so to be careful."

She slid into thong sandals and dropped heart-shaped sunglasses into her jute bag. Colleen had gifted Maeve the sunglasses with gold and pink lenses, a fun reminder of rose-colored glasses.

"They suit your outlook on life, Maeve," her friend had said.

As they walked into the lobby arm in arm, Maeve steadied Edward.

"Bonjour Monsieur and Mademoiselle Perfect Match." A bubbly Pierre stood behind his desk. "How is your ankle today, Monsieur Newell?"

"Excellent. Please thank your staff for the flowers and good wishes." Edward put an arm around Maeve's shoulders. "My lovely lady takes excellent care of me."

Maeve felt the heat rise to her face. She wasn't Edward's "lady," although he did make her feel that way.

"*Tres bon*, monsieur. Carissa will meet you by your fishing boat. Such an exciting day, oui, to fish in our beautiful waters?"

"I don't swim," Maeve reminded him.

"Swimming isn't required," Edward said. "You just need to stand at the railing of the boat and catch a fish."

"How?"

"I'll teach you."

"Your boat is a yacht charter, mademoiselle," Pierre said, "and I assure you it is spacious and stable. Below decks is a shower, toilet, table and a small galley kitchen. Jules Baduoin will be your captain. He founded the original sea company here on the island and you will appreciate his knowledge of Corsica."

"I confess, I'm nervous," Maeve said. "I've never sailed on a fishing boat, or any boat, for that matter."

"Jules is an outstanding captain," Pierre reassured her. "And remember to be back at the hotel in plenty of time because dinner is at—"

"Not tonight." Edward raised a hand. "I'm taking my luv somewhere extraordinary."

My luv. Truly, she needed to say something to stop him from using that term, but the warm feeling in the pit of her stomach told her she wouldn't.

Don't be silly, she told herself, examining and reexamining the meaning of a harmless saying. Brits used the word *luv* all the time.

Pierre riffled through a stack of papers on the reception desk. "Achille asked the chef to add to tonight's menu herb-fed veal cooked with olives, prepared as a stew. And, as always, the champagne of your choice."

Before Maeve could respond, Edward said, "As much as we enjoy the resort's food and Maeve adores her champagne" —he nudged her with his elbow—"I have a special surprise arranged for her."

Pierre leaned forward over the desk. "What is the surprise, monsieur?"

"Good luck trying to drag it out of him," Maeve said. "If the topic is surprises, Edward is as close-mouthed as a clam."

"Now I am even more curious." Pierre couldn't indulge his curiosity, though, as several tourists flooded the lobby, chattering loudly, and Nigel rushed by hauling a cart of heavy luggage.

Leaning to the side to talk to them around the guests rapidly lining up in front of his desk, Pierre gestured to a Bonaparte Resort van idling at the curbside. "Our driver will take you to Porto, a brief twenty minutes from our resort. Enjoy your day."

As they turned to the door, Edward sent Maeve a teasing smile. "You can relax on the sundeck while I fish."

"I thought you said you'd teach me how to fish?"

He clasped her hand and led her outside. "Just say the word and I'll teach you anything you want to learn."

A sunlit day greeted them, and the trees swayed gently in the heady, hot breeze. Spindles of green plants poked through the cracks in the cobblestones.

Promptly, she drew her sunglasses from her bag.

"Your fair skin will burn in minutes with this tropical sun," Edward remarked, putting on his aviators.

"The hat will shade my face." She patted the top of her head. "And I plan to slather on sunscreen."

They arrived at the dock in Porto a short while later. Carissa and a cameraman met them by the fishing boat.

Before Carissa could suggest a pose, Edward pulled Maeve into his arms and gave her a swoon-worthy kiss. "I want to spend every minute with you," he whispered.

"Just think," Carissa said, coming between them. "Next month you two will probably be on the front page of the Perfect Match website as a resounding success story." Her zeal was so contagious they all laughed.

Edward placed an arm around Maeve's shoulders. "I fancy that idea," he said, and she couldn't hide her smile.

"Everything's all set on the boat," Carissa said. "We'll just take one more picture before you get on board. And if you catch a fish today, Jules will let us know. We'll arrange to have your fish cooked in one of our partner restaurants."

After the final photo, Edward stepped away when his cellphone rang. "It's my sister, Karen," he mouthed to Maeve. "I won't be long."

"You're not joining us?" Maeve asked Carissa as she waited for Edward to finish his call.

"No. There are too many tourists visiting the island. August is high season, and I'm booked for the rest of the day."

She adjusted her huge dark sunglasses and flipped back her blonde ponytail.

Edward clicked off his phone and rejoined them. As they boarded the boat, Carissa called out, "You two have fun!"

"Sure," Maeve muttered. "She gets to stay on land."

Edward laughed out loud. "And you get to stay with me." Lightly, he kissed her forehead. "Even better, I get to stay with you."

Jules, their captain, greeted them at the helm and introduced himself. His bronzed face and arms were weathered by years in the sun, his hair thin and sun bleached, his hands rough. His smile revealed a few missing teeth, but he had an easy way about him.

"My boat is over thirty feet long, allowing me to easily steer into the coves," he said, his English heavily accented. "Come take a look. I'll be in the wheelhouse once we begin."

As they pulled away from the dock, nearby boats bobbed and then settled as their wake passed. Georges, the deckhand, welcomed them on board. Edward and Maeve stood behind the console while he stored their gear below deck.

Maeve insisted on wearing a life vest. Edward did the same.

Georges set up the fishing equipment on the casting platform and pointed out where the safety gear was located. "We will begin with vertical fishing and drop the decoy to the bottom of the sea." He attached a wriggling squid to a barbed hook and passed the fishing rod to Maeve.

Edward gave her a teasing bump with his hip, then set up his own fishing rod. "May the best fisherman win."

"It's not a contest," she admonished. "And I thought you were going to help me."

"To a man, everything is a competition. I'm here if you need me, though."

"That's a relief, although it sounds more like you're saying, 'Every man for himself.'"

"Are you both amateur fishermen?" Georges asked, then pointed out a blue dolphin on the starboard side.

"So beautiful." Maeve stared at the dolphin in wonderment. "If you count the fact I've never fished in my life, Georges, then I'm a definite 'aye.' I don't know about Edward."

Edward shrugged. "I'm no expert, but I enjoy all sports. Well, most at least. I'm on the fence about golf."

Once Jules got to a sheltered fishing ground and shifted the boat to neutral, Georges went up to the bow and anchored the boat so it stayed in position. Then he guided Edward and Maeve to an open spot on the platform near the railing and they dropped their lines. Above them, buzzards nested in amber rocks, contrasting with the scrublands and wild countryside and sea. A picture-perfect postcard, Maeve thought.

"What types of fish can we expect to catch?" Edward asked, keeping a keen watch on his fishing rod.

"Snapper, tuna, and sea bream live in these waters, as well as barracuda," Jules said as he emerged from the wheelhouse. He grabbed a bottle of water from the cooler and took a swig. "You never know what will emerge at the other end of your line."

"Does that mean I might catch something big?" Maeve leaned her rod against the railing, then let out a shriek when it immediately jiggled.

"You must be fast, mademoiselle!" Jules told her. "Hold tight and start reeling."

"What am I reeling?" She bent over, laughing so hard she couldn't catch her breath. Then she tugged.

Thanks to Edward, she reeled in a snapper weighing eight ounces, and was informed by Jules the fish was not a keeper, because keeper fish were ten ounces or more. He handed her a hook remover. She removed the hook and, grimacing, released the fish back into the water.

"All by myself." She wiped her hands and smiled at Edward.

"You're a born fisherman, luv." He grinned at her and then turned to Jules. "Carissa mentioned on-site restaurants can prepare our catch for lunch. What happens if we don't catch anything?"

"No worries, monsieur. We packed spuntinu, a Corsican sandwich. You may eat at the dinette in the cabin belowdecks."

Edward nodded. "Maeve's an expert sandwich maker. Supply her with two pieces of bread and she's on her way."

She laughed. "Maybe not Corsican sandwiches."

Although she and Edward reeled in five more fish to enthusiastic applause from Jules and Georges, they opted to assemble Corsican sandwiches on deck and stay there to eat, appreciating the view of water and the uninhabited countryside.

After lunch and several bottles of water, Edward sat on the stern's swim platform and dangled his legs in the water. He patted to a spot beside him. "Sit with me, Maeve."

The waves rolled in lazy arcs, foaming as the water broke against a stretch of sugar-sand beach. A school of sunfish swam past. Among the large white-flowered sea lilies growing alongside the rocks, the shore was alive with gulls.

She settled on a beach towel beside him.

"Can I ask you something?" he began.

There wasn't the normal teasing amusement in his voice. "Aye," she said, curious where this was going.

They sat together through a long moment of silence.

"What?" she prompted.

"Why are you still single?" He steepled his hands. "A woman like you is usually engaged or married."

"I don't understand."

His gaze probed hers. "You know, a beautiful, desirable woman who puts everyone before herself. You should've been snatched up long ago."

"As a barefoot, dutiful wife?"

"No. As a woman who should be loved and cherished."

Heat flooded her cheeks. She studied her hands clasped on her lap. "I've been in relationships with men. They never work out."

Memories of the way her last boyfriend, Finbar, had ditched her came to mind. She'd thought he loved her, but it had all been a facade. It was odd how much you could care for someone and feel chock-full of honey and gladness, and then experience only a twinge of a former connection when the name resurfaced.

Edward was watching her, no doubt evaluating her distant stare, her flat tone. He brushed the sweat from his eyebrows and scanned the water. "Care to skinny-dip with me?"

She gave a bark of surprised laughter. He obviously was attempting to draw her out of her apparently upsetting memories with his scandalous suggestion.

"Was it that obvious?" she asked.

"I don't like to see you upset."

"Are you joking about the skinny-dipping?" She added an eyeroll before her gaze darted to Jules and Georges standing in the wheelhouse. Gaily, they both waved.

"Nope." Edward shrugged, mischievously, but an inner beam lit his gaze.

She acknowledged the other men's waves and then glared at Edward. "Neither am I joking. My answer to your question is an absolute no!"

"It was worth a try."

"Don't tell me you actually thought I'd agree."

"No, I didn't. If anything, you're proving to me what kind of woman you are."

"And what kind is that?"

"A woman of integrity. A woman I admire more each day."

Before she could reply, he shrugged off his T-shirt and pulled his phone from the pocket of his trunks, placing them both on a lounge chair. Then he grabbed the pull buoy Georges had supplied, smoothed a kiss on her temple and climbed down the swim ladder.

"I swim like a Spanish mackerel and I'll be right back," he said.

"What kind of fish is a Spanish mackerel?"

"A fast one."

"What about your ankle?"

"The pull buoy will support my legs and I'll use my arms. This isn't a workout. It's purely recreational."

With that, he eased into the crystal-clear depths of the Mediterranean, positioned the pull buoy between his knees, and swam the freestyle stroke. The cool splashes on her feet were a welcome relief from the heat, and someday, she pledged, she'd learn how to swim.

Drawing the line at skinny-dipping, though.

When Edward swam back to the boat, he toweled off, playfully shaking his hair so that drops of water sprayed her.

Perspiration trickled down her arms. The day was hot, the sun was high. Finally, heat won over modesty, and she yanked off her straw hat and coverup. Her bikini—a white scalloped top and flirty black bottom featuring dangling ties—showed off her slim figure. The saleswoman at the gift shop had assured Maeve the bikini was simple and chic.

"Wow." Edward dropped his towel and gave a low whistle.

"You're stunning, luv." He hesitated, seeming to grope for words. "Are you aware you're drop-dead gorgeous?"

When she started to protest, he caught his arm around her waist. As he pulled her close, his wet bare skin brushed against hers. He didn't try to kiss her, simply holding her as they stood by the railing. Together they admired the craggy peaks of les Calanche Cliffs breaking against the azure skyline.

"Do you approve of my swimsuit?" Suddenly shy, she couldn't quite meet his gaze.

"I love everything about you. Surely you must know that by now." He smiled at her. This rising heat in his cheeks was more than sunburn, and a smoldering desire darkened his eyes to a deep forest-green.

"I couldn't find a one-piece swimsuit in my size," she said.

He brushed a soft kiss against her lips. "Exceedingly good fortune for me and every other male on this island."

Georges came back out on deck to raise the anchor, and Jules navigated the boat into a cove that offered dappled shade and a waterfall gushing from a mountain. After Georges dropped the anchor again, Jules came out of the wheelhouse and eyed Maeve appreciatively.

"*Tu es belle*, mademoiselle."

"Merci." Her cheeks were most likely scarlet by now, and she caught Edward frowning at Jules.

"Georges and I are grabbing an afternoon snack before we go back to the harbor," Jules said, snagging another bottle of water.

"Take your time," Edward called after them as they made their way below deck. He laid his towel out beside hers. "Finally." He gathered her in his arms and kissed her long and hard. "Privacy."

She wedged a hand between them to create some distance. "You know how I feel about being alone with you.

Especially when you look at me with an expression of such … I don't know how to describe it. With such interest."

"Interest is a good start," he said. His breath caressed her cheek, rousing feelings she couldn't define. "Remember you can trust me."

"Aye." She did trust him. But when she was with him, she didn't trust herself.

He bent his head. "Then you realize the affection I feel for you."

She couldn't tell if he was serious or joking, but she was here for several more days, and it seemed senseless not to enjoy her time with him.

Slow and steady, he kissed her again and she couldn't help herself, gliding her hands across the hard contours of his bare chest. She heard his soft gasp as he pulled her closer and gazed into her eyes. She stood on her tiptoes and slipped her arms around his neck. Mouth to mouth, they kissed as if the sun could whirl away and reappear, taking its time before reality revisited.

When the kiss ended, he grinned. "I'm very, very glad I came to Corsica."

"And why are you grinning like a Cheshire cat?"

He grabbed for his phone on the lounge chair and typed a text message. "Because our Wednesday adventure isn't over. I've arranged for us to travel someplace special for dinner this evening."

"Several of the Corsican guidebooks featured restaurants tucked in straw huts near the sea. They sounded divine. Are we going to one of those?"

"Somewhere better."

"Will the resort drive us there?" she persisted. "Several of the restaurants are an hour away."

"We're merely forty-five minutes from our destination."

He kissed her again. "And I suggest you dress up for a one-of-a-kind occasion."

She peered at the sun, a ribbon of muted orange as it began its descent. "As if there's enough daylight left after an ideal afternoon like this to do anything better."

"We don't need daylight." He brushed his lips up and down her neck. "And our evening will surpass everything we've done so far."

"Edward," her tone spun over the boyish edge of his, "where on earth are we going?"

At his wide grin, a sizzle of pure attraction coursed through every inch of her.

"We're flying to France." With that announcement, he turned off his phone and set it beside his T-shirt on the lounge chair. "The pilot is fueling my company's private jet to take us to my favorite restaurant along the French Riviera."

CHAPTER 8

"The French Riviera?" Colleen repeated, when Maeve rang her the following morning. "You flew in his private jet to dine in one of the poshest restaurants on the French Riviera?"

"Actually, it's his family's private jet."

"Okay, that settles it. Does Edward have any brothers?"

Maeve gave a hoot of laughter. "He has a sister who seems to have an exemplary business sense, and two younger brothers. But what's the craic with Colin? Are you on-again or—"

"Off-again," Colleen completed. "He wasn't my type, anyway. He didn't want to work, but he certainly liked to spend money."

"If he didn't work, where did he get his money?"

"He wanted to get it from me. Thus, I told him to crack on. He was locked half the time anyway."

Drunk.

Maeve rested on her king-sized bed against a pile of fluffy silver pillows. Despite arriving back at La Bonaparte Resort in the early morning hours, she'd hardly slept. Who could

84

sleep after dining in the courtyard of an eighteenth-century French mansion beneath one-hundred-year-old trees, seated across from the most handsome man she'd ever seen, a man who'd never taken his admiring gaze off her?

Cozy and unpretentious, the painted-wood brasserie was tucked down a cobblestoned lane and brimmed with old world Provencal charm.

Edward had been impeccable in sharply pressed black trousers, jacket, and white shirt. His sea-green eyes created a jump in her heartbeat each time she met his stare. His thick black hair was tousled by the ocean breeze, and his strong hands had held hers. The intimate round table had been covered in blue and yellow French linens, a pattern depicting sea and sky, Edward explained. He went on to say that there were close to thirty three-star restaurants in France, and he'd chosen his favorite to share with her.

The menu had featured five courses, and she savored the earthy taste of a beetroot topped with caviar, a delicacy she'd never sampled. Edward preferred the home-baked baguettes and dessert trollies rolling between the cozy tables.

Often, he leaned across the table to brush a kiss along her ear. A full-out laugh had erupted from him as she told a story about her animated, eager-to-please pug. He described a particularly memorable camping trip he'd taken with his lab.

In fact, they talked all evening, hardly pausing to catch a breath.

It was the romantic setting, she decided as she gazed at his face.

But no, it was more, much more. She was seriously falling headfirst in love with him. And it was reckless and divine.

No. She pushed her contemplations back and attempted to regroup. Too many emotions, too quickly. Surely, she was smart enough to keep thoughts of love away.

Her heart, however, didn't want to heed her hesitations.

What was it about this charismatic man? No matter how much time they spent together, they never ran out of conversation. They declined the expensive French wines and Champagnes the waiter suggested, settling on sparkling water. *Sorbet aux framboises*, a mouth-watering raspberry sorbet, had been served between courses to "cleanse the palate and stimulate the appetite."

Edward hadn't brought up his business, or his family, or resuming his London lifestyle.

His life in the real world.

She hadn't spoken of Ireland. She'd begun to wish her days, her nights, her week here in Corsica spent with Edward, would never end. When she was with him, her difficulties slipped to a far corner of her mind.

After dinner, they strolled the perimeter of the restaurant's courtyard, tracing a whiff of honeyed aroma to hollyhocks growing upward against the stone walls.

He'd stood close behind her, his arm around her waist, indicating tiny hilltop villages and ancient paths spiraling to the sea. Lifting her hair, he inhaled a deep breath and nuzzled her neck. "I love the scent of your hair."

"You mean the smell of fish from our boating adventure?" she joked.

"No, I mean your fragrance, like an exotic, sparkling lemon." He kissed her mouth and then murmured, "I like the flavor of your lips too."

"Really? Like beets and caviar?" She still wasn't sure when he was joking or when he was being flirtatious. She only knew she was enchanted by him, and close to losing her heart.

He dotted her face and her lips with soft kisses. His mouth was still moist from their meal, and he tasted of sugar-coated raspberries and sparkling spring water.

Someday, he promised that he'd show her the nearby

towns, for he knew the region well. They would take their dogs and wander narrow cobblestone streets flanked by fields of lavender and acres of yellow sunflowers. She could immerse herself in history, and he'd savor the quality of a quintessential French lifestyle—watching old men play lawn games and fishermen hauling in their catch of the day, or buying bread fresh from the bakeries in town.

Lately, he murmured, he'd been longing for a slower pace in order to truly appreciate life.

"I'd like you to see my home near London," he finished.

She hesitated. Save for Corsica and America, she'd never traveled outside her safe little Irish world where brogues were melodic, laughter was frequent and friendly pubs stood on every corner.

Then she looked into his eyes and agreed with a definite, emphatic, "Aye."

They were both reluctant to end the magical night, and lingered over cappuccino and raspberry macarons at an outdoor café. On a side street, the music of an accordionist playing a French melody had drifted down to them. They faced their chairs toward the sea, holding hands, watching the colors of midnight pool on the harbor's waters.

And there she told him everything, her mother's continuous flings with men who lived in a kip, a dump. About her absentee father. About facing up to her worries and fears and even guilt because Owen was sick and she wasn't.

She also revealed her stints in low-budget movie roles as an extra, the need for time-consuming rehearsals for a scene that lasted only a minute or two, and the constant rejections that came with show business.

"Persevere," he encouraged, tapping her coffee cup with his, and she instantly felt right as rain.

"Can this all be real?" she murmured, half to herself.

"What?"

"The French Riviera, this night …you."

He flinched, then tipped up her chin and said softly, "Very real, luv."

Why had she told this man, whom she'd only known a few days, so much about herself? Because, she rationalized, of the surreal setting in a romantic new country, along with the emotionally charged days. Or perhaps, although she'd stated on her profile she was a good listener, he was better— asking questions, genuinely relating to what she said and offering to help her in any way he could.

Of course, she had refused his help. She'd learned long ago to stand on her own two feet, to rely on no one else.

Although, with Edward she had no barriers, and he had applauded her milestones as she outlined her university years and how she'd landed her job as purchasing agent for Merrimac.

"I'll teach you another French term," he said, leaning back in his chair.

"What is it?"

For a split-second he said nothing. Then he leaned close, so close his breath touched the strands of her hair. *"Joie de vivre."*

"Which means?"

"The joy of living. The French believe life should be about food and drinks and sharing special occasions with the most important people in your life."

His voice had become oddly rough, and he briefly closed his eyes. She studied him in his moment of vulnerability, trying to decipher all he meant.

And then she struggled to think at all, because poignant tears clogged her throat.

He opened his eyes and she smiled into his searching gaze, realizing the same emotion coming through him had also passed through her.

That connection again. Deeper and more pronounced as the minutes flew.

"Was dinner romantic?" Colleen interrupted Maeve's musings.

"More than you can ever imagine. We sat outside in a courtyard that overlooked a harbor on the Cote d'Azur. Women entertained on their cruisers, wearing cropped trousers and carrying basket bags, very Grace Kelly looking. Edward recognized several socialites and celebrities.

"All glitz and glamor on the French Riviera. What did you wear?"

"My black lace sheath dress and ankle-strap sandals."

"The three-inch stilettos?"

"Aye." Maeve stared out the window wall of her bedroom, which framed the varying landscapes, from the glorious ocean to the rough mountain ranges. "And Edward promised next time we visit the Cote d'Azur, we'll take a drive along the coast and he'll show me his family's resort there. And he said we'll enroll in a cooking class. He doesn't cook, and I'd love to learn how to prepare French cuisine and pair meals with wines and Champagnes."

Edward promised ...

Next time ...

He said ...

There was a pause and Maeve feared the call had been disconnected. "Colleen?"

"I'm here. Look, Maeve, are you certain a guy like him is single?"

"Aye. He told me he's married to his work."

"Then believe him. Regardless of his obvious interest in you, he's off-limits. Even if you wanted to continue seeing him after this week, a long-distance relationship never works. So don't fall too hard, promise? It took you months to get over Finbar."

Maeve rubbed her forehead. "No worries, Colleen. I'm a practical woman and I'll be home soon enough. Who can blame me for appreciating every magical minute?" She rolled to her stomach and studied the morning sunlight, endless pinks and reds spreading across the sky. "Edward and I are exploring more of the island today. There's a strand of beach for sale, and his company might be interested in acquiring the property. If a hotel is on site, Merrimac will want a report on it as well." Maeve came to her feet and cupped the phone to her ear. "See you on Sunday, all right? After I land in Dublin, I'll visit my mom and Owen and then ring you."

"I'll expect every single solitary detail about you and Edward."

After assuring Colleen she planned to begin working once she'd viewed the available beach property, Maeve clicked off.

Edward texted her shortly afterward, telling her to enjoy a lazy morning. He was dealing with an unforeseen business problem and needed to talk with Karen, and he would pick her up at one o'clock.

Regardless of her notes from earlier days, Maeve didn't work a smidgen, too busy propping her feet up on the balcony and appreciating the variegated blues of sea and sky.

Several hours later, Edward rapped on her suite door, calling out, "*Bonne après-midi*. Good afternoon, gorgeous." He strode out onto her balcony and leaned down to kiss her.

"*Bonne après-midi*," she agreed.

"Your French is improving every day. Did you miss me this morning?"

She smiled and gazed into his eyes. "Of course."

"Did you think about me?"

"A little." *More than a little.* "Is this a solo interrogation?" She pulled back. "Did you think about me?"

Lazily, he fingered an errant wisp of her hair and wound it around his finger.

"I never *stop* thinking about you, Maeve."

A trill of heat started in her belly and she shivered. "Well, I'm ready."

"Almost." He glanced at her sandals. "I recommend you pack a soft-soled flat shoe and wrap for later."

She poked through her closet and emerged with both. "Later? Why?"

"Another surprise." He unzipped the canvas tote he carried and combined her shoes and pashmina wrap with his loafers and tan sweater. Without further explanation, they headed to the lobby.

In response to Pierre's queries, Edward explained the location of the beachfront acreage his company was interested in purchasing.

"Ah, oui." Solemnly, Pierre parroted the location. "The former owner went bankrupt, and the property is an excellent opportunity."

"My resort may compete with yours once we're up and running." Edward inclined his head in a half-joking nod. "Can I persuade you to come work for me?"

Pierre straightened even more, if that were possible. "Monsieur, if I am honest, non. No other hotel can compare with this beautiful resort." He swept out his arm toward the grandiose lobby, the ornate chandelier dangling above the broad staircase. "Will I leave all this? Never."

"I appreciate your loyalty, Pierre, but my offer is always open. If not this resort, then any my company owns." With that, he tucked Maeve's hand into the crook of his arm. "Ready for Corsican Adventure Day Four?"

A smile touched her lips, and she pretended she had to think about it. "Perhaps."

In all honesty, she couldn't wait to spend every waking second with him.

As they turned to leave, Pierre enquired, "I trust your dinner last evening on the French Riviera was memorable?"

"How do you know where ..." Maeve interrupted her own question with a head shake. Pierre made a point of knowing the goings-on of all his guests.

"Tonight, we will plan on you both dining on our terrace at eight?" Pierre continued.

"Sorry." Edward held up a hand, a déjà vu of yesterday. "I've made other arrangements for us."

A flutter of anticipation went through her body. Maeve glanced at him uncertainly as she tossed her jute bag over her shoulder. "You're positive I'm dressed appropriately for our mystery date?"

He examined her patterned red silk halter top and tailored capris. On impulse, she'd donned her crystal chandelier earrings, the same pair she'd worn to dinner the night before. As his affectionate gaze returned to her face and lingered, she felt that familiar flush creep up her body.

He wore sandals, striped linen Bermuda shorts, and a kelly-green golf shirt. Utterly impervious to a gaggle of women gawking at him from the bar, he guided Maeve out the lobby's front door.

The hotel van reached the strand of beach in the predicted twenty minutes, and Edward directed the driver to wait for them.

The area proved stunning, the azure sky fringed by dozens of precipitous mountain peaks. Out on the water, sails on colorful fishing boats snapped in the wind, and gleaming steeples atop medieval church towers crowned the nearby hills.

One by one, she and Edward peered inside a row of

deserted whitewashed cottages with deep-orange trumpet vines twining up their sides.

Edward took off his sunglasses. Shading his eyes, he gazed at the sea. "What do you think of the property, Maeve?"

As always, the water was as turquoise as a precious jewel, the sand a soft golden brown.

"Ideal for a resort," she said, "though I'm not keen on the notion of spoiling the beach with a high-rise."

"My company will evaluate the target. I'm certain regulations are in place to preserve the natural habitat. Regardless, my intention is to enhance the Corsican character."

"Your intention? What does that mean?"

"It means my assurance. You can count on my word, much as I can count on yours." He gave a firm nod.

She saw the glint in his gaze, the joy of the hunt. This was another side of Edward, the keen-eyed businessman she hadn't glimpsed before.

"And your company?" he was asking. "If the deal went through for Merrimac, you'd probably receive better bids from your hospitality supplier."

"You mean J and J? Aye, they'd probably offer me competitive pricing on their lighting and seating, but I've never been involved in a project of this size. Granted, I assume Merrimac's intentions are the same as yours." Reflectively, she exhaled. "Still, my vote is to keep this property undisrupted. Once it's gone, it's gone. I'm obviously not a good businessperson, aye?"

"Development is good … sometimes." He gazed at her thoughtfully. "Although I don't want to be the guy who overdevelops this gem of an island any more than it already is."

His phone buzzed, and pensive, he glanced at the text

message. His mood changed, and he grinned widely, shoving his phone into his pocket. "Ready for another surprise?"

He grabbed her hand and hailed the Bonaparte van. When they settled into the backseat, he asked the driver to take them to the Bonifacio marina.

"Edward, hold on, where are we going?" Maeve asked. "Your adventures are always special, but this time I want an answer before we arrive."

"We're going to a yacht party."

Rapidly, she blinked, the concept of a yacht party as elusive as traveling to the moon. "What in the world is that?"

"People host a party on their yachts and we're invited."

"Please don't tell me," she ran a hand along her hair, which she'd styled in an elegant low bun, "you own a yacht as well as a private jet."

"No." His smile turned potent. "My friend Bentley, the guy who signed me up for Perfect Match, texted this morning with an invitation and he just confirmed. He's anchored near the harbor. He wants to meet you and said he invited someone."

"Who?"

"Don't know. A surprise, I imagine."

"Is he friendly with any movie stars?" Maeve's eyes widened, and she fidgeted with the edge of her halter top. "I'm not dressed properly. What do I say, how do I act?"

"You act like yourself, Maeve. And if you're unsure, remember you're a professional actress." He gave her hands a reassuring squeeze. "Believe me, just be yourself and you'll charm the entire ship. Now, the first thing you do when you board is to remove your shoes. Or—" He held a finger to her lips before she objected. "You wear the flat shoes you brought."

The van dropped them off at the harbor's tip where a limo tender waited. Timothe, the tender's helmsman, provided a hand onto the boat, pledging to deliver them dry and comfortably. A mega yacht with flashing lights was anchored in the distance.

Overcome with awe at the size of the yacht, she couldn't utter an audible word.

She only knew Edward would stay beside her, soothing her discomfiture. The knowledge made her happy and calmed her nerves.

As the tender sped toward the yacht, they relaxed in its roomy interior with the glass roof open. The wind blew swiftly across her cheeks, snatching wisps of her hair. A filmy mist teased the fringes of the horizon as day eased to dusk. How novel this all was, every hour filled with giddy excitement and heady experiences. With Edward's arm around her, she settled into the saddleback leather seat for the quiet, smooth ride.

When they reached the mother ship, as Edward had named it, he opened his tote, and they switched their shoes.

"Time to charm," he said. He wrapped the pashmina around her shoulders to ward off the sea breeze and steered her onto the limo's stern.

So much of what she'd learned about him was in his little, thoughtful gestures, his constant consideration of her comfort. The way he held doors for her, or took her wrap, or stood respectfully until she was seated. The way he paid attention to her, supportive and encouraging. All these traits were a matter of course for him, because he was a perfect gentleman.

And she recognized that every one of those qualities were the foundations of a true, loving relationship.

She took a deep breath of salt-laced air and squared her shoulders. "Aye. I'm ready."

"Courage, luv. Remember, these people are my friends." He took her hand as they boarded. "I assume my sister Karen will be here. This morning she informed me she'd intended to snag an invitation if it was a go."

As if on cue, a woman in an off-the-shoulder chiffon who had an astonishing resemblance to Edward walked toward them. After embracing his sister with an affectionate hug, Edward introduced Maeve. Then he excused himself to speak with an older man who had shouted "Bonjour!" to them.

"He's one of my father's associates in Nice," Edward explained to Maeve. "I won't be long."

Karen watched her brother walk away, and then turned her crystal-green gaze on Maeve.

"He's very attracted to you," she remarked.

"Who? Edward?" Maeve's mouth opened, but for a second, nothing came out. "Why would you say that?"

"Because he talks about you nonstop."

Maeve felt her cheeks blaze with color. "We've only just met. We were placed together through a dating agency. Neither of us really wanted to be here."

"Well, it's obviously an on-target arrangement for you both. Trust me, he's love-struck. I watched him when you climbed aboard—the way he looks at you, the heat in his gaze —" Karen fanned her face. "My brother and I talk about business every day. Since he arrived in Corsica, he's spent maybe five minutes talking hotels, and then the rest of the time he talks about you."

The women remained in sociable silence for several beats while Maeve mulled this information over. Then she shook her head. "You're wrong, Karen."

"When it comes to matters of the heart, I am right. And you are in love with him."

"How do you know?" Surely, Maeve thought, her feelings for Edward weren't that obvious. Or were they?

"Because I am a woman, so I know you." Karen enhanced

her statement with a breezy smile. "And I am his sister, so I know him."

After a brief pause, Maeve said, "The Perfect Match meter is running out."

She tried not to think about it, because thinking caused a sadness she didn't want to face.

Her arm through Maeve's, Karen steered her over to a buffet table ladened with appetizers and scooped up a slice of cantaloupe. "No. Edward will continue to pursue you until he wins you. When he loves, he loves deeply—Our mother, our family …" Contemplative, she dabbed her lips with a cloth napkin and sighed. "When we lost our mother, our father's grief was so painful to see. Our parents were very much in love, you know. Up till today, Edward hasn't given his heart to any woman. Now he has."

"Sometimes I don't know if he's joking or sincere," Maeve said cautiously.

"Men usually try to hide what they feel most passionate about." Karen shrugged. "He was our family's rock when our mother got sick. After she passed, he closed up and immersed himself in business. I sense you will be good for him." She greeted a passing friend with a French air kiss. "I'm without my husband tonight and enjoying a girl's night out before I divorce him," she explained to Maeve. "When I heard about Bentley's party, I rearranged my schedule so I could be here. I was curious to meet you, and now I am satisfied." She hugged Maeve tightly. "I hope we can become good friends. I'm the only woman in my family, floundering in a sea of males and I need another woman's voice. I hope it's sooner rather than later."

Edward helped Maeve walk across the huge teak deck and through the midst of chattering partygoers.

"And how did you find my sister this evening? She's a veritable chatterbox."

"She's lovely," Maeve replied, "and very friendly. Did you know she's divorcing her husband?"

"I've heard all about it. And from what she's explained, I can't fault her."

"Edward!" Automatically, Edward looked up and spotted Bentley, their host. He'd noticed Bentley had anchored his yacht just far enough out to sea, so that his guests needed to board another boat to reach it. Typical Bentley and his flair for the dramatic, never to be outdone. Competition was normal between the two men, and Edward acknowledged that he often encouraged it. However, it could go on and on, and truthfully, the money, the bragging rights, meant nothing to him. He much preferred Maeve's warm body pressed to his, her languorous gaze after he'd kissed her, the simple pleasure of hearing her melodic Irish brogue.

"And this must be your Perfect Match," Bentley said. His pale-blue gaze leveled on Maeve, and he didn't bother to hide his curiosity. Without warning he seized her hands, pulled her close, and welcomed her with a triple cheek kiss. "I'm Bentley, Edward's friend from university."

She took a step back. "Hello, Bentley. I'm Maeve."

"Look at this beauty! Edward certainly aced this week with the likes of you, chérie. From the little I got out of him, I knew he was smitten and chose to see you for myself. I'm a twit for entering his name on the Perfect Match website instead of mine. Come with me." Before Maeve could protest, Bentley drew her hand through his arm and started to move away from Edward with her. "Everyone wants to learn all about you."

"Kindly take your hands off my luv," Edward said in a low voice.

Bentley turned back. "Your *luv?*" His blond eyebrows rose in laughing irony. "Point taken, mate. I knew things moved fast in our circle." He scooted back, hands up, palms out, and then clapped a hand on Edward's shoulder. "Sorry you suffered an ankle sprain. The fellows had a jolly laugh—you being an outdoorsman and a lovely, petite Irishwoman coming to your rescue. If it weren't for her, you might still be strung on a high cliff atop Corsica."

Standing close to Maeve, Edward felt himself stiffen at Bentley's jibe. He stiffened further when Bentley took up two flutes brimming with Champagne from a passing waiter. He offered one to Edward and one to Maeve.

"As you well realize, I don't drink," Edward said shortly.

"And the lady?" Bentley demanded.

"While I can't speak for her, I know she is exceedingly fond of Champagne."

Maeve hesitated, a quiet longing in her gaze as she eyed the crystal flutes. "Not tonight. Sparkling water is fine." As she declined, she glanced at Edward.

Bentley caught the glance. "Surely, Maeve, you don't ask this Ivy League bloke for permission?"

"I assure you, Bentley." She slanted Edward an impudent smile and brushed her hand across his. "I can speak for myself."

Edward grinned and wrapped his arm around her. "And I can verify that fact."

"So, Maeve." Bentley gulped down half of one of the glasses of Champagne. "Edward mentioned you're in the hotel business. What's the name of the chain you own?"

She laughed. "I'm merely one of the purchasing agents for the Merrimac Company in Ireland."

"A purchasing agent?" Bentley frowned, and then turned to look over his milling guests.

The well-dressed men and women, in a dazzling display of the moneyed at ease, snickered and chattered, toasting each other with champagne flutes in one hand and plates of shrimp cocktail in the other.

"Follow me, Maeve." Bentley turned on his heels, seemingly assuming Maeve would join him. When she didn't, he looked back at her, frowned again, and started forward anyhow. Over his shoulder, he hollered, "There's plenty of liquor. I'll catch up with you two later."

"Thank you, Bentley, but we don't—" Maeve inclined her head, although Bentley was well past them.

Several nearby guests turned to study her, no doubt wondering who she was, and Edward tightened his hold around her. He felt her push out a breath and set her shoulders straight as she sent the curious group a straightforward smile.

His heart gave an unexpected lurch. She might be taken aback by all this, but she would never cower. Not his Maeve.

Completely unassuming, she was a natural in his often-times unnatural world of excessive abundance. In a world where being seen at all the right places with all the right people was more important than a person's character or deeds, she was the opposite, preferring to carry herself with modest dignity and grace.

"We'll find an open spot by the railing and I'll fix you a plate of food," he said.

"Always the gentleman." She beamed at him. "Even with a hurt ankle that doesn't seem to bother you in the least anymore."

"It still hurts a little, so you can continue to fuss over me." He grinned and was rewarded with her smile in return.

"Notwithstanding, I'm a new man because of your judicious care."

"Notwithstanding and judicious in one sentence? You're beginning to sound like Dawson Yates."

He laughed out loud. She looked gorgeous tonight. Her beautiful face and radiant smile brought a surge of longing, crumbling his world weariness. There was an irresistible charm about her, an effortless sparkle that beckoned men closer.

His quick look around confirmed that men were, indeed, staring at her.

Well, he'd make sure each one of them realized that Maeve was his and his alone.

A nagging thought brushed the corners of his mind.

Since when? Hadn't he declared that first night at the hotel that Perfect Match was a game that would end when their allotted week did? Yet when he held her and she snuggled against him, he knew she fancied him. And he fancied her.

Silently, he shook his head.

Fancied was such a trite term.

He wanted her, more than anything or anyone. He wanted to hear her engaging laugh every day of his life, to banter and talk seriously, to fill her days and nights with the same pleasure she gave him.

He wanted her to care for him as much as he cared for her.

Because he loved her.

Love?

The thought swung him impressively back on his heels, so much so that Maeve turned to peer at him.

Love? Absolutely not. No man with a milliliter of sense fell in love with a woman he'd known for less than a week.

But here she was, beautiful and alluring, and he couldn't

deny his feelings when his heart skipped a beat every time he looked at her. He was completely and utterly in love with her.

"Edward, are you all right?" Dark with concern, her gaze held his. "Does your ankle hurt, just after you've finished telling me you're okay? I won't be telling you that you should've brought your crutches, although you should have."

"I'm fine, luv."

He couldn't look away from her. Her silk top clung to her slender curves. Her subtle fragrance of citrus and sunshine perfumed the air. She looked, well, smashing and quite enchanting.

"Honest. I was joking about the fussing." His gaze veered to the buffet and beverage stations situated at strategic points along the deck. Dismissing his ankle with a wave, he asked, "Do you care for stuffed mushrooms or beef Wellington?"

Two hours later, Edward was relieved at a break from the swarm of outwardly good-natured acquaintants who had converged on them. He'd sensed a malevolence toward Maeve from a few women when they learned she *worked* for a company and didn't *own* one. He knew Maeve heard the occasional murmurs of "Gold digger" from the way she gripped her hands together, and he had to refrain from lighting into the insensitive women.

"Ignore them, luv," he whispered at one point as she curled her fingers tightly around his.

"I feel so unsophisticated," she confessed. "Like I'm a silly girl playing dress-up in a world where I don't belong."

"You're perfect. It's them. They don't belong in your world." He sealed his assurance with a solid kiss.

Unlike the women, the men evidently agreed with Edward, showing a decided interest in Maeve. She accepted their over-the-top compliments, their gallant offers to fetch her plates of chocolate-dipped strawberries or a dozen French lemon tartes. With a flattering flush in her cheeks, she conversed with wit and self-assurance.

Now that they were finally alone for a beat, Edward asked if she wanted more sparkling water.

"Aye. Then can we please leave?" She sampled a last bite of strawberry, her mouth enticing, as rosy as her red-patterned blouse.

Her sparkling water forgotten for a minute, he pressed a kiss to her lips. "The problem with a yacht party is we're stranded until the boat heads back to the dock. Since I figured Bentley would try to strand everyone out here until dawn, I hired our tender for the night. We can call for him to come back for us at any time."

Edward circled back with her water a few minutes later, not pleased that Bentley had taken his place next to Maeve. The two of them were looking out at a calm sea. No waves, no white crests. Midnight and moonless, although the ocean mirrored the glitter from the yacht's masthead and sidelights.

"Did you twist an offer of marriage from him yet?" Edward overheard Bentley ask Maeve before taking a gulp of whatever alcohol was in his high ball. Probably vodka.

Maeve kept her head high. "You've known Edward since your university days, so certainly you must realize no one can 'twist' anything out of him."

Edward wedged himself between the two of them, forcing Bentley to step away.

"Back so soon?" Bentley said. "I was just asking Maeve about your relationship."

"And Maeve wasn't naïve enough to presume she had to acknowledge your disrespectful question."

Undeterred, Bentley inquired, "So … this match arrangement. Do you two share a room?"

"We each have our own suite," Maeve answered. She

cloaked a pleading glimpse at Edward, then pointedly stared at the shore. It was high time they got off this yacht, she was silently telling him.

"You're not sleeping together?"

"Maeve and I only met a few days ago," Edward said.

"That's never stopped you before."

Edward's heart pounded a furious beat against his ribs. Weighing his options, he decided not to end the night on a fistfight. With a slight inclination of his head along with a bland smile, he changed the subject. "Before we joined you tonight, Maeve and I discovered a beachfront property for sale."

"Isn't the Newell family wealthy enough? Why purchase another resort for Penelope and Edward?"

"Or for Merrimac," Maeve put in. "My company is also searching for hotel property."

Bentley sniffed his glass. "You'll have little say. You're only a mere purchasing agent."

"Aye," she agreed. "Although J and J Hospitality has saved Merrimac thousands of dollars through the years because of their low bids."

"I've used them on occasion," Bentley said. "They've never allowed my hotels reduced rates."

"Maeve drives a tough bargain for the best price when dealing with suppliers for hotel seating and lighting." With a playful grin, Edward raised her hand to his lips for a fleeting kiss. "She's a skillful buyer."

Bentley slammed back the rest of his drink. "I'm sure Merrimac's accounting department is delighted, although we all like to generate a substantial profit in our businesses."

A limo tender was speeding toward them. Edward wondered if maybe their driver, Timothe, had read Maeve's mind. But it wasn't theirs, so he pulled out his phone to text Timothe to come get them.

Maeve had also noticed the tender. "Are you expecting one more guest, Bentley?" she asked. "If so, he or she has redefined the phrase 'fashionably late.'"

Maeve pulled her pashmina tight around her shoulders, and Edward tucked the ends around her waist. When had the air turned so bitter? he wondered, surveying the sky. All the stars were hidden behind a haze of black clouds. Friday, he remembered, called for showers.

Impatient for Timothe to arrive, he shifted. He was in a hurry to go back to the restful, familiar confines of La Bonaparte Resort, instead of being trapped with Bentley. Somehow, he vowed, he'd make tonight up to Maeve and atone for the behavior of his insolent friends.

"It is a she," Bentley answered Maeve. "And *fashionable* is her middle name."

"Did she travel far?" Maeve asked as the tender pulled up alongside the yacht and a woman stood up. She wasn't the only one watching as the stunning, sensual woman in a form-fitting silver dress boarded the yacht.

Edward keyed in Timothe's number again, willing his phone to connect faster.

"She sailed from Italy, chérie," Bentley answered. "She summers in the Italian Alps and winters in Milan. Her family owns a conglomerate of high-fashion clothing stores, and she is the sole heiress."

Edward swallowed hard, trying to get rid of the odd taste in the back of his throat.

"Italian *Vogue* will undoubtedly discover her, if they haven't already." Maeve watched as the woman glided toward them, waving and calling hello in Italian to various people. "Is she your super-model girlfriend?"

"Edward," the woman called. "I've missed you!"

Edward's head snapped up, and he found himself the center of too many people's attention. Smug Bentley, acquaintances watching avidly, and wary Maeve. And Davinia, her smile as stiff as her tight dress.

"Why haven't you answered when I've texted and called?" Davinia closed the distance between them. "I thought you fell off the planet this week, Edward."

Stillness reigned, split only by the subtle motor of Timothe's tender finally nearing the yacht.

"Didn't he tell you, Maeve?" Bentley's mocking tone cut through the awkward silence. "Davinia DeVito is Edward's sweetheart. They've dated for years and are practically engaged."

CHAPTER 9

*J*ust as the Corsican weather report had predicted, Friday morning brought rain. Maeve peered out the sliding doors leading to her balcony and watched a seabird take flight. Sleek and chilly, the face of the red cliffs looked unfriendly, shadowed by a fierce downpour and framed against an empty bleak sky.

The previous evening, after Edward swiftly boarded the tender behind her, he'd responded to her frosty silence by asking if he could explain himself.

Although she'd felt all the color drain from her face when Bentley had introduced Davinia as Edward's sweetheart, she'd listened to Edward. Still, the shockwave of his betrayal had thumped the breath from her.

She had no reason to feel that way. She had known the entire week was for an online dating promotion. Nonetheless, tears had burned the backs of her eyes, and she'd studiously avoided his gaze.

He'd dated Davinia, he said, although he certainly wasn't engaged to her and didn't plan on ever marrying the Italian heiress.

As the waves vibrated against the speeding limo, Maeve had sunk against the seat and tried to weigh whether or not he was lying. More important, she questioned why his relationship with Davinia mattered so much to her.

Once they reached shore, Edward opened his canvas bag and slipped on his tan sweater, then offered her shoes to change. "Bentley's gone too far with his so-called practical jokes," he muttered. "When we attended university, his pranks were silly. Now they're mean-spirited and hurtful."

"Aye." Her anger had bubbled to the surface, and she let it loose. "Life's a joke to idle men who have more time and money on their hands than they know what to do with.

"Are you referring to me?"

"Perhaps." She heard the Irish temper in her voice and couldn't even it out.

"Is this all because you're jealous of Davinia?"

Bristling at the gleam of satisfaction in his gaze, she didn't answer, chiding herself for refusing to admit the truth, even to herself. She was relieved the tender had reached shore, and gathered her shawl more tightly around herself.

"Well, in any case," Edward said, "I'm jealous of you." Before she could step onto the deck, he planted a firm kiss on her lips. "That's why I kept you within an inch of me all evening."

"You don't trust me?"

"I don't trust other men. They'll all lose their hearts to you, as I have, Maeve."

She'd believed him, his assurances, the slumbering passion in his eyes when he'd kissed her. Hadn't his sister said that Edward was taken with her? Surely Karen, of all people, knew him better than most. Besides, one glance at Bentley, his thin lips and silver-tongued manner, was all the assurance Maeve needed.

Bentley liked trouble. Some people did, she supposed.

So, the tight clutch in her stomach had dissolved. She'd woken in a good humor, and was perched on a stool in her suite's efficiency kitchen, savoring the breakfast tray that had been delivered to her room. Buttery croissants, fresh melons topped with crushed mint, and café—a shot of espresso in a gleaming patterned cup. Achille had also included a special recipe, a goat cheese omelet compliments of his "Tata Jeanne."

Relishing a bite of the sweet fruit, she glimpsed her sandals, crusted with sand, by the door and her bikini hanging on the back of a living room chair. These were wonderful reminders of her beach holiday with Edward.

Finishing her breakfast with a sigh of contentment, she showered and then dressed for the day in flared woven capris and a white cotton eyelet top. Finally, it was Friday and time for their visit to the Bonaparte Museum—an excursion she'd looked forward to all week. Carissa had planned a tour for after lunch, so she still had a few hours to fill.

Barefoot, she padded to her well-appointed bedroom. She'd already spent several minutes applying eye make-up, something she rarely did. She wanted to look pretty for Edward, especially after seeing the stunning Davinia and the high-powered style of the women who populated his exclusive, wealthy world.

And, she wanted to polish off the bumpy edges of the persistent disbelief in her mind, shake off her feelings of inadequacy in this elite universe she'd scarcely fathomed before this week.

Perched on a generously proportioned armchair, she picked up a hairbrush. After her shower she'd braided her freshly-shampooed hair to encourage more waves. Now she shook her hair free of the braid and pulled it to her crown in a messy bun.

Her cell phone rang, with Colleen's name and number

drifting across the screen.

She'd texted Colleen the night before, summarizing her evening on Bentley's yacht, including her perception of the underhanded way he'd operated, and her encounter with Davinia DeVito.

As the phone rang a second time, Maeve peered at her watch. Midmorning in Ireland. Odd time for Colleen to call because she never rang anyone when she was working.

"Maeve?" Colleen's voice sounded distant when Maeve answered. "This is Colleen from the purchasing department."

Maeve paused. "I know who you are, Colleen."

"Where are you?"

"I'm in Corsica. Why?"

"You need to come home to Ireland immediately."

An icy chill burrowed deep in her bones. "Owen? Is he all right?"

"Owen is fine. Mrs. McShea instructed me to ring you. In fact, she's standing over my shoulder while we speak."

"What's the craic, Colleen?"

"Is Edward Newell in the hotel business?"

"You know the answer." Maeve set down her hairbrush and stood. "Aye."

"Well, the Merrimac Company is being charged with collusion. Did you and Edward visit a beachfront property yesterday?"

"I told you, remember?"

"Aye. And an informant rang Merrimac with the details this morning."

"Who? What details?"

"We're assuming it was Edward or one of his associates who rang. They're demanding J and J Hospitality offer their hotels a better discount on lighting and seating—the same bidding price they extend to Merrimac."

"What's the name of the hotel chain?" Weighted by

doubts, she heard the strain in her voice. "Are you certain it's Penelope and Edward?"

"They didn't say. Our accounting department is checking receipts and accounts payable. Maeve," Colleen whispered into the phone, "if J and J raises their prices, Merrimac may no longer be profitable. We could all lose our jobs if the hotel folds."

No. Maeve squeezed her eyes shut. Edward would never undermine her and betray her trust to save money on supplies—although the savings for his business could tally up to hundreds of thousands of dollars.

Still, the suspicions wove a ribbon of confusion through her mind. She kept her eyes closed, trying to recall her conversation with Bentley. If he attempted to discredit her position, why didn't he realize her savings didn't include numerous stocks and bonds and trust funds to fall back on? She lived paycheck to paycheck. Yet she could see him in her mind's eye, smirking, finding her predicament amusing.

"Get on the next flight out of Corsica," Colleen said, "and you'll arrive in Ireland before the work day ends. Hold on." Maeve recognized their boss's high-pitched voice in the background, then Colleen was back. "Mrs. McShea said for you to come directly to the office. She also wants to review all the reports you've compiled this week. She hasn't received anything. Is your internet working?"

Before Maeve could answer, Colleen hung up.

Breathless, she booked a return flight to Ireland at an exorbitant last-minute rate, rang for a taxi, and then packed quickly and charged out the door. A stinging throb pinched her side. She held her hip and ignored the rapid-fire questions Pierre shot at her when she reached the lobby. He gestured to a taxi waiting curbside to bring her to the airport.

"Mademoiselle, does Monsieur Newell know you are

leaving?"

"No."

"Forgive my intrusion into your privacy, but shouldn't you notify him? Today is your outing to the Bonaparte Museum."

"Another time, Pierre." Although she knew there would be no other time. "Please tell him I was summoned back to work."

She wasn't lying, really. All sense of right and wrong and proper and inconsiderate was pushed to the back of her mind.

Disconcerted, she flicked a glance around the lobby. When had the hotel become so crowded? And why did every guest seem to hover so close to her?

She breathed in and out. The lobby was too small.

Pierre was typing something into his computer. "You live at 101 Fourth Street in Dublin, oui?"

"Aye."

"You are obviously in a great hurry. I will arrange a taxi for you when you arrive in Dublin."

"Thank you." It was too much effort to explain to Pierre that she was reporting to Merrimac first. She'd tell the taxi driver once she landed.

Somehow, she kept her gaze confident, her expression neutral. But how could she explain to Amy and Dawson … to Edward?

Why, oh, why had she been so short-sighted? Prideful of her responsible behavior, she'd lost her head and her heart to a man she'd known for only a few days. And now she and Colleen might lose their positions and their incomes.

And what would happen to the other Merrimac employees if the company closed? Jobs in Ireland were hard to come by.

Her throat tightened around a sob. She'd never belonged

here in Corsica, milling with affluent people whose lifestyles were as distant from hers as shooting stars. She hadn't considered the practical, only the impossible. In her dream castle, her life and Edward's could be woven together.

She'd now received the proof that she'd been very, very wrong.

Wheeling her suitcase behind her, she shuffled down the stone steps of the resort. Fortunately, Pierre had abandoned his position behind his desk and hurried after her with an enormous umbrella, saving her from the drenching rain.

"Mademoiselle, is there anything I can do?" he asked as the taxi driver stowed her suitcase in the trunk.

"No, you've been wonderful, really."

"Mr. and Mrs. Yates? Shall I ring them?"

"I'll contact Amy and arrange to reimburse any booking expenses for today and tomorrow, as well as whatever else I might owe."

How she'd repay, she couldn't comprehend, because there was no money in her bank account. The driver opened the back door for her, and she started to step in. Pierre kept the umbrella over her, which left him in the rain. Almost instantly, his tawny-colored hair, lacquered in its familiar side-sweep, was plastered to his head. His shoes, normally gleaming to a fine black polish, were soaked. Funny how she'd never noticed the lines on his thin face before, nor how misplaced he looked outside of his setting behind his desk.

"Come back to our paradise soon?" he said.

She shook her head, sorrow in her farewell smile. "Au revoir, and merci beaucoup, my dear friend."

As she bent down to slide into the taxi, she noticed a stray feather from some seabird lying on the cobblestoned street. She picked it up, knowing she'd never see the exotic island of Corsica again, the wild thyme, the ancient stone ruins, the awe-inspiring coastline.

Or Edward. The man she loved.

And then she cried as the taxi drove away. Silent hot tears. To keep herself from shattering, she focused on the white lace of the Mediterranean crashing to shore.

Edward may have insinuated his way into her emotions, but she was through thinking about him and his trendsetting friends who believed they could manipulate ordinary people.

Well, he and his friends wouldn't be controlling this woman.

Inhaling a sturdy breath, she opened the taxi's window and released the feather into the wind. An updraft carried it for a short while before it plunged to the ground.

As a fat, stubborn tear fell down her cheek, she concentrated on her last view of Corsica—a moss-covered fountain beside a statue of Napoléon, shade-loving vines climbing over trellises, a random scooter skirting past the taxi.

Determinedly, she brushed the tear away. "Good-bye, my beautiful island, and my Mr. Right. Somewhere in my heart, I knew I could never live in your world."

But she had hoped. And she had dreamed.

What had she expected? An affair of the heart? A story of true love?

She sank her head in her hands and told herself not to cry.

She cried anyway, because she just couldn't govern her feelings anymore.

* * *

THE REMAINDER of Friday passed in a blur, but at last Maeve was in her flat and putting the kettle on for tea. She'd been fired from Merrimac, although she'd denied any wrongdoing. Collusion wasn't even part of her vocabulary. Nevertheless, her company was small and couldn't take any chances going up against giant corporations. Besides, Mrs. McShea had pointed out when Maeve had gathered her personal belongings from her cubicle, Maeve had bunked off from work from when she'd landed in Corsica to when she'd returned to Ireland.

Maeve hadn't denied the charge. How could she?

Saturday dawned with the same angry, relentless rain that had saturated Corsica the day before. She drew on a sweater, pulled on a pair of wool socks, and boosted a fire in the hearth. Crinkles sat at her feet, gamely wagging her tail.

"I thank the good Lord every day since I found you at the rescue shelter." She picked up her dog and was rewarded with a light lick on her cheek. What was better than a dog's love—their kind hearts, their devotion for their owner, their companionship?

With Crinkles in her arms, she padded to the window and gazed out at the somber sky. Then she turned and scanned her tiny living room. Her flat seemed so quiet without her brother.

Despite her mother's questions when she'd stopped in the previous evening, Maeve had been thrilled to see her brother looking healthy and content, and had lifted a prayer of thanks.

To top off her success in avoiding any inquiries concerning Edward, she'd noted that her mother and brother were getting along brilliantly.

Holidays would be lovely this upcoming year with their small family of three. But first came the end of summer, followed by autumn. Even now, she could feel the warm season pushing away, easing into shorter days and gloomy, unfriendly nights.

She crumpled into her comfortable chair by the fireplace and Crinkles cuddled beside her. Tightly, she closed her eyes, but that didn't stop the tears that streamed freely down her face.

By afternoon, the rain had settled to a slow and steady drizzle. Deciding soup would ease the sadness in her chest, she put a chicken on the stove to boil, one she'd bought on her way home the night before. She managed to eat only one bowl, but that left ample servings for her mother and brother.

Feeling revived by the soup, she unpacked her luggage. Routine stabilized her, strengthened her and kept her mind and hands busy.

In the deep quiet of afternoon when the shadows of the day lay long, her doorbell jangled. She glanced at herself in the living room mirror. Her cheeks were streaked with tears, her eyes watery and red. Swiftly, she groped for her handkerchief and dabbed at her face.

"Remember me?" Colleen shouted from the other side of the doorway. "Why haven't you answered my texts?"

Maeve opened the door. "Sorry." Seeing her best friend's questioning gaze, she stuttered, trying to catch her breath. "T-tea?"

"Are you all right?"

"I'm grand." Her voice cracked, only slightly, but enough for her friend to take hold of her hands.

"Then why were you crying?"

Maeve averted her gaze. "I've excelled in crying ever since I left Corsica."

"That's absurd. I've known you since we were in primary school, and you never cry." Colleen hung her jacket on a kitchen chair and wiped the water drops from her glasses. "The rain is cold and nipping through me like prickles of ice. I'll say aye to that cuppa tea."

A handful of minutes later, with tea and a plate of biscuits in front of them, Colleen perched across from Maeve in

Maeve's cramped kitchen. Crinkles rested beneath the table, crunching a treat Maeve had fetched from the cupboard.

"I'm sorry about your job," Colleen began.

"Fortunately, you're still employed, so a wee bit of fair play there." Maeve chewed on the corner of a biscuit, then drank a mouthful of tea. "Monday will come around soon enough. In the help-wanted section of today's newspaper, one of the shops on Fifth Street is hiring. It's only a block away, so I could easily walk."

"With your experience, you'll find a good job. You're a brilliant purchasing agent."

Was she? Instead of answering, Maeve poured her friend more tea.

"The tea is good and hot." Colleen boosted her sugar intake with another lump. "Maeve …"

"Aye?" Maeve dropped back in her chair and stared at her steaming cup.

"Have you heard from Edward?"

Just the sound of his name sent a beat of pure yearning through her heart and relit a fire she didn't think she could ever extinguish. She missed him so much.

She gulped a lungful of air. She couldn't lie, not to Colleen. Desperately, she tried to hide the catch in her voice. "He's left numerous phone messages and texts."

Realization emerged in Colleen's cornflower-blue gaze. "Which, I'm assuming, you haven't answered. And I can see by the look on your face you're in tatters …"

Maeve bent her head to hide the welling tears, but not soon enough for the keen-eyed Colleen.

"You fell in love with him, didn't you?"

"Don't be ridiculous." Chin lifted, Maeve offered Colleen a quivering smile. "I met him a week ago."

"Love isn't measured by time. Why haven't you answered his messages?"

"I can't."

Colleen pushed back her teacup, then clicked her French-manicured fingernails on the table. "Why not?"

"Because I wouldn't know what to say."

Because it would distress her too much to hear his voice.

Maeve flopped back in her chair and gripped the armrests. "If only you knew how he lives. What we imagine to be the lifestyle of the rich and famous doesn't even come close."

"You've told me all week about it, remember?"

"Then you should understand."

"I understand, all right. You're a coward."

"Me?" Annoyed, Maeve flashed her friend a pained stare.

"Oh, don't get your dander up." Colleen threw up her hands and studied a crack in the ceiling. "You're ignoring him because you're upset, although none of this is his fault. We both know it was Bentley."

"Perhaps."

"Perhaps? *Perhaps?*" Colleen jerked from her chair, stalked two paces, then pivoted. "Surely you don't doubt Edward. I did some digging on the internet last night. Bentley's a big front and a slow back. From what I gathered, he's feigning a family wealth that isn't there anymore."

In a deceptively casual tone she hoped would dissuade Colleen, Maeve refuted, "None of this matters anymore."

"I didn't know you were so ridiculous." As if too furious to continue, Colleen went back to her tea, dissolved a handful of sugar cubes in it, and stirred vigorously. "If you want to break it off with Edward, tell him straight on."

Maeve gave a half laugh. "There's nothing to break off."

"Umm, nothing except your starry-eyed week together." Colleen shoved Maeve toward her laptop computer sitting on a narrow kitchen counter. "Tomorrow, book a ferry from Dublin to Holyhead. Then take a train to London."

"Surely you're joking?" Maeve's eyebrows jerked up. Her fingers clenched into small fists. Momentarily irrational, she almost agreed with Colleen before they settled back on their chairs.

"What's the story then, Maeve?"

"Sorry, I just don't know anymore." Maeve rubbed her arms. "Besides, I don't have any money."

"Merrimac gave you two weeks' severance. Use part and go directly to Penelope and Edward's main offices."

"I don't know where they're located." Maeve groped for a better answer. "Perfect Match didn't disclose any personal information."

"Thank goodness, again, for the internet and your brilliant techie friend." Colleen slipped a paper from her pocket and slid it across the table to Maeve. "Here's the address."

At a loss for words, Maeve frantically considered how to end a conversation that would only lead to more pain if she pursued it.

"Doesn't he have enough, Colleen?" She reached down to pet Crinkles. The dog represented security and everything good in her world. Crinkles nosed her fingers, hoping for another treat. With a heavy sigh, Maeve put her head in her hands. "Shouldn't living an exorbitant lifestyle surrounded by more worldly goods than anyone can comprehend be plenty for one man?"

"He doesn't have you."

"As if that matters to a rugger bugger like him. I'm certainly not showing up on his office doorstep like a pining puppy."

Colleen took a bite of biscuit and washed it down with tea. "I suppose if I was in the middle of a misunderstanding like you are, I'd see things the same way."

"This is more than a misunderstanding."

"Is it?" Colleen held up a hand. "Please, just to stake my argument, let's presume he's in love with you."

Maeve opened her mouth to object, and Colleen stopped her with a sardonic head shake. "From what you told me about all his special surprises, even a cabbage would realize how much he cares."

"No. It's better if I move on and forget him." Maeve surged to her feet and began clearing the table. "Sooner or later, I'd make a right moron of myself and—"

Colleen crossed to her and gave a tight hug. "I doubt he'd spend all his time, money and energy on a woman he cares little about."

A torrent of clashing emotions swept through Maeve as Colleen determinedly continued. "At least give him the benefit of listening to what he has to say."

"And then what?" Maeve swiveled and busied herself at the sink. She'd tried so hard to numb her emotions, and then here had come Colleen. "He'll give me a little pat on my head and send me on my way? I'll be mortified."

Colleen plunked her hands on her ample hips. "Your pride may need to suffer."

"I can't. I just can't."

"All right, then stay here in Ireland. And when you read about his engagement to Davinia what's-her-name in the Dublin papers, let me know your thoughts then."

"Maybe I'll consider ..." Maeve studied her worn hardwood floor. She needed time to sit somewhere quiet and reflect. Surely Colleen could understand.

She met her friend's gaze. "I'll—I'll wait a while first."

"Which will be even more uncomfortable as the weeks go by." Colleen plucked a slice of chicken from the pot of soup and chewed slowly. Rounding back to Maeve, she poured on a brilliant finale. "Provided, of course, he hasn't wed Davinia in the interim."

CHAPTER 10

The following morning, Maeve peered out at another wet drizzle streaming down her bedroom window. Her entire flat felt damp. She opened the top drawer of her bureau and sniffed the lavender-scented sachet she'd brought from Corsica to place with her clothes. Tied with a purple satin ribbon, the sachet's fresh, appealing scent reminded her of France.

She closed the drawer, the fragrance too painful a reminder. She'd been a foolish woman who'd chosen to believe fantasy over reality. End of story.

Still, her flat was so forlorn. After showering and getting dressed, she grabbed a history book and sat by the fireplace. Crinkles snored at her feet, easing her loneliness. She'd mindlessly turned several pages of the book before she gave up, realizing she couldn't concentrate on sixteenth-century war tactics.

Save for a cuppa tea, she didn't have the heart for breakfast. For lunch, she'd heat up a bowl of the chicken soup. Perhaps she'd be hungry by then.

As she stared out at the dreary day, her cellphone pinged.

The sound almost sent her to her knees. If it was Edward, should she consider answering his text? These unmanageable feelings for him were so chaotic and powerful.

Uncertainty collided with hope as she picked up the phone to check the screen.

Instead of Edward, an incoming email from Carissa was emblazoned with the title, "Remembrances of a Perfect Match created in Corsica."

Telling herself she should resist the temptation to open the file because her heart couldn't afford to be any more broken, Maeve tried to stop herself and failed.

Slowly, she read and reread Carissa's email.

'Hi Maeve,

Sorry you left our beautiful island so abruptly. We miss you and Pierre says bonjour.

Hope you enjoy these remembrances of Corsica.

Your Perfect Match specialist,

Carissa'

Maeve scrolled through the attached photos, and a sting of longing grew in her chest.

Orange lilies in her hands, the first photo was of her and Edward cuddling at the foot of les Calanches Cliffs. Aye, they'd agreed to act for the cameras.

But had they been acting?

Maeve changed the picture size and zoomed in on Edward. His expression was tender as he gazed down at her, which she hadn't noticed when he'd kissed her.

She rewound the day in her mind, remembering his smile when they'd perched on the rocks with the splendor of Corsica before them.

"Wouldn't you agree, Maeve?" he'd said. *"We get along so well. We're never at a lack for words. Perhaps we are made for each other."*

Edward.

She wanted to cry out, to weep. She squeezed her eyes shut, running her fingers across the phone screen to touch his face, willing the tears not to fall.

The second photo was taken in his suite. He'd worn his fleece shorts and Snoopy T-shirt. She was dressed in his chambray shirt, which would have fallen to her knees if she hadn't tucked the edges into her jean shorts. The orchids portrait was propped behind them, and she held a bouquet of Corsican lilies. He was leaning against her, exaggerating his injury. She recalled how the closeness of his hard, toned body had made her feel both faint and lighthearted.

And that feeling had never changed.

She scrolled further to the third photo, taken of them beside the fishing boat. Edward, with his midnight-black hair, startling green eyes, graceful dark eyebrows. He'd surprised her with a passionate kiss, prompting Carissa to exclaim they were the Perfect Match success story.

"I love everything about you," he'd said when there were anchored in a cove. *"Surely you must know that by now."* And then he'd brushed a soft kiss on her lips in that intimate way he had.

A fist squeezed so tightly around her heart she could hardly breathe.

Edward.

She breathed out a shaky sigh. So many remembrances— vaulted stone doorways in ancient towns, the pattern of boat silhouettes and fog on the harbor, their enchanted night on the French Riviera. As they'd sauntered hand in hand, he'd pointed out the trellises decked in climbing vines, and low marble fountains with basin rims broad enough to sit on.

Stop, she scolded herself. Her home was hundreds of miles away from him, from Corsica, from La Bonaparte Resort.

Her Irish lifestyle? Well, that was a million miles away.

Stubbornly, more memories resurfaced.

Remind me to never quarrel with you.

And she'd assured him she would do anything to avoid a conflict.

But did that mean surrendering, giving up the man she loved?

Her mouth fell open. Her head came up.

With an exclamation, she embraced the fluttering in her chest. Grabbing her cellphone, she rang Colleen.

Maeve kept her tone steady when Colleen picked up. "Will you watch Crinkles for me?" she asked.

"Job-hunting on a Sunday, aye?"

"No, I'm hoping you'll spend the night. I'm off for a wee bit of traveling."

"Really?" Maeve heard Colleen's short intake of breath. "Where?"

"To London."

"You're a fine thing, you know that?" Colleen started whistling the tune from a familiar Irish jig. "I'll be there in twenty minutes."

Decision made, fine or foolish, Maeve bundled her hair up.

She could do this.

She kept her chin up while she organized an overnight bag with her necessities. She was prepared.

Besides, Colleen was right. She couldn't be so spineless as to ignore Edward simply because it upset her to be near him. How could she be so petty? If she admitted the truth, didn't she owe him that same honesty? She'd have a straight conversation with him, then head back to Ireland the following morning.

Still, when Colleen arrived at her flat, Maeve confessed she was panic-stricken and already considering canceling her trip. "Why don't we go into Dublin centre and window-shop instead?" she'd suggested.

Colleen gave her a hard stare. "Finish Perfect Match the way you started, optimistic and determined. Be the woman he fell in love with—the self-assertive woman who always rises in hard times."

* * *

MAEVE CALLED a taxi to the Dublin port, where she'd booked a round-trip ferry ticket between Dublin and Holyhead.

Rain was still falling, and she pulled up the hood of her bright-red rain jacket as she walked swiftly into the terminal. A glance at her watch assured there was enough time to collect her ticket and enter the check-in point with maybe five minutes to spare.

She saw the broad-shouldered man immediately, because he was tall among the crowd, striding purposefully across the ferry dock and wheeling a small leather carry-on. In his other hand, he held a bouquet of orange lilies. He paused, questioning a deckhand, then nodded his thanks and passed through the tollbooth.

She tilted back her head, devouring every inch of his handsome face. Steps wide, she ran toward him.

"Edward!"

He looked around. He didn't see her at first. And then he did.

"Maeve!" He found her in an instant, started to reach for her, but then stopped.

"Why are you in Dublin? In the ferry terminal?" Warily, she scanned his face for a sign he'd come on business or for some other reason that had nothing to do with her. Or perhaps he'd come to berate her for not answering his calls and to tell her he never wanted to see her again.

He smiled into her curious gaze. "I just got off the Holyhead ferry."

Holyhead.

"Maeve. Luv." Heartbreakingly handsome, he set down the flowers and held out his arms. She dropped her bag and rushed into his embrace.

"I missed you so much," he murmured against her lips.

"I missed you too." She molded herself closer, fearful that if they came apart, he would disappear; and the painful torment of losing him would become a void she'd never be able to fill.

When their kiss finally ended, his arms tightened possessively, and he rested his chin on her hair. He paused a moment, waiting for their breathing to smooth out.

Slightly, he drew back. "Where are you headed, Maeve?"

"I intended to travel to London. But not anymore." She tossed a rueful glance toward the Holyhead ferry, which was signaling its departure with three horn bellows.

Understanding dawned in Edward's eyes. "For me? You were going to London to see me?"

"Aye."

He lifted her off her feet and whirled her around. He was a man with the power to carry her.

"I was bound for 101 Fourth Street," he said.

Her address.

"Maeve?" He studied her face. "How did you know I'd be here? I didn't tell anyone—"

"A very fortunate coincidence. Call it happenstance, call it fate." She called it the benevolence of a loving God and whispered a prayer of thanks. She and Edward had nearly missed each other.

"Why did you decide to come to me?" His gaze never left hers. "You've ignored all my messages."

She twined her hands around his neck, aching with

desire, unconcerned about showing her feelings. "My friend Colleen made me understand that I needed to face my emotions."

"And they are?"

"I love you, Edward, and I won't deny it another second." She lay her cheek against his hard chest, loving the sound of his solid heart beating. "It's crazy, I know, because we've just met and—"

"And I love you." Sincere, honest emotion deepened his words. "Maeve Doherty, I love you very, very much."

She looked up at him and it was all there. His love, his desire for her.

Suddenly awkward, he bent down and handed her the bouquet of orange flowers. "These are for you. I know you loved the lilies in Corsica. They're a bit bent, I'm afraid ... I can get you another ... Maybe roses instead?"

"Lilies are perfect." She took the flowers and breathed in the heady scent of Corsica. "Thank you." Her voice broke. "Thank you."

As a drizzly Dublin day neared to evening, they sat on a bench under an overhang and gazed out onto the harbor. Passengers embarked and disembarked on infinite journeys, leaving behind wet footprints on the docks. Some smartly dressed, some simple and plain.

The lilies were on her lap, their carry-on bags at their feet.

Then, since neither of them had eaten, they took a taxi back into the city to Maeve's favorite coffee shop, The Ground Café. With her bouquet of lilies on the table, they enjoyed lemon scones washed down by the coffee of the day, a rich, strong brew.

"All that separated us was a ferry ride," Edward said. "Why didn't you respond to my thousand and one messages?"

"I was wrong. And I shouldn't have blamed you for the actions of your friend." She lowered her head, twisted her hands together. It was difficult to speak. "I lost my job. Merrimac charged me with collusion and jeopardizing our accounts with J and J Supplies by giving out bidding information. Someone called my company Friday morning to report me. That's why I had to go back immediately." She looked up. "I'm not dishonest, Edward. Merrimac's been fair, and I'd never do anything to damage them."

He took her hands in his, squeezing lightly, offering his loyalty. This persuasive, powerful man was her champion, and the thought made her proud.

"You've done nothing wrong." He paused. "Do you think Bentley …?"

"Aye. At least I assume."

"I'll find out the truth." He stiffened, a cold, flinty expression crossing his face. Then he nodded, his gaze gentled. "So now you're jobless."

"Aye, although there's a prospect posted in the Dublin paper that I'll reply to tomorrow. The business is a short block from my flat, so I can walk there." She tilted her head. "How did you know my address?"

He looked out the nearest window. "The rain's stopped. How about a walk?"

She agreed, and as they stepped outside, she looked up. Far to the east, a bell tower tolled. Her gaze drifted, resting on the first star of the evening.

He didn't answer and hung an arm around her shoulders. The fierce downpour had stopped. Dusk had turned a dove-gray sky into reddish hues. Low clouds were parting for a clear, bright nightfall.

The same question plagued her and she turned sideways to face him. "Edward, you said you were headed to Fourth Street. How did you know my address?"

He slipped an arm around her waist. "How did you know mine?"

"I didn't. Colleen gave me the address to Penelope and Edward headquarters. I hoped someone would be there on Sunday."

He smiled. "Rest assured, that someone would be me. Karen separated from her husband and flew off to Australia on the family's private jet to spend the weekend with a man she met on Bentley's yacht."

"I wish Karen luck."

He sighed. "At the rate she's going, she'll need it."

Maeve shook her head. Then she stopped walking, forcing him to stop and regarded him frankly. "Edward, how did you know my address?"

"First, I planned to contact the Perfect Match people. The … the …" He snapped his fingers.

"Yates. Dawson and Amy Yates."

"Right. But I didn't need to. Pierre gave me your information."

"He'd never agree to give out my personal information. He's much too professional." She raised a dubious eyebrow. "Would he?"

"For love, he couldn't refuse." Edward chuckled. "And …"

"And?"

"Begging."

"You begged him?"

He shrugged. "I added bribery. I offered him a head concierge position at Penelope and Edward's Nice resort at double his current salary."

"Surely he didn't accept."

"Actually, he did, so his future is ensured." Edward bent his head to capture her mouth in a long, leisurely kiss. "As for your future … I don't see that you'll be needing to apply for that job. I can offer you a much better one … Mrs. Newell."

Her heart gave a lurch. He announced his intention so simply, so like him. She understood his core, trustworthy and giving, and she treasured it. Treasured him.

He took her into his arms and gazed into her eyes, which were quickly filling with happiness. "You haven't answered my question," he said quietly. "Will you marry me?"

Her answer began in her spirit as her heart filled with too many sensations to name. In a perfect French accent, she whispered the chorus from "La Vie en rose," that when a man takes her in his arms, she sees the world through rose-colored glasses.

Edward held her closer. "Your quote on your dating profile."

"Aye. You remembered. And Pierre taught me how to say it in French."

"So I noticed. Now, will you marry me?"

"Aye. Because I love you very, very much."

"And I love you, Maeve Doherty."

This was love, and perfection. And the man who held her in his arms was her Perfect Match.

THE END

A NOTE FROM JOSIE

Dear Friends,

Maeve is set in Corsica, a charming French island located in the Mediterranean Sea.

I've always been fascinated with traveling the world and exploring new places. In my spare time, I appreciate "armchair vacations" and watch popular television shows in exotic locales. Several shows were an inspiration for my story.

You'll find that Maeve is a strong Irish heroine. Intelligent and competent, with a beautiful, gentle spirit, she sets out on the adventure of her dreams.

And of course, Edward, the hero, conquers his own challenges.

Despite their differences, and the fact that their economic situations are worlds apart, I found that the characters "clicked," and I loved writing this book!

It is my hope that you will enjoy this heart-tugging romance, and come to embrace the supporting characters. Your feedback means a great deal to me, and I'd appreciate your review.

Maeve is available in ebook, Paperback, Large Print Paperback, Hardcover, and Audiobook.

Happy Reading!

My Spotify Play List for Maeve is here.

Josie Riviera

Love "Irish" books?

Be sure to read:

A Chocolate-Box Irish Wedding

Oh Danny Boy

1-800-IRELAND

Irish Hearts

TATA JEANNE'S CHEESE OMELET RECIPE

Ingredients:

- 6 eggs
- 5 oz of fresh ricotta cheese (or goat cheese)
- handful of fresh chives, green onion, or mint
- 1 tsp. grated garlic
- 1 tbsp olive oil
- salt
- pepper

Instructions:

Break the eggs in a bowl and beat. Season with salt and pepper.

In a non-stick pan, heat olive oil. Add grated garlic and fry. Pour eggs over and cook.

Spoon in ricotta or fresh goat cheese. Let ingredients settle until cheese is warmed.

Sprinkle with fresh chopped chives, green onion, or mint. Enjoy!

ACKNOWLEDGMENTS

An appreciative thank you to my patient husband, Dave, and our three wonderful children.

ABOUT THE AUTHOR

Josie Riviera is a USA TODAY bestselling author of contemporary, inspirational, and historical sweet romances that read like Hallmark movies. She lives in the Charlotte, NC, area with her wonderfully supportive husband. They share their home with an adorable shih tzu, who constantly needs grooming, and live in an old house forever needing renovations.

To receive my Newsletter and your free sweet romance novella ebook as a thank you gift, sign up HERE.

Become a member of my Read and Review VIP Facebook group for exclusive giveaways and free ARCs.

To connect with Josie, visit her webpage and subscribe to her newsletter. As a thank-you, she'll send you a free sweet romance novella directly to your inbox.

josieriviera.com/
josieriviera@aol.com

ALSO BY JOSIE RIVIERA

Seeking Patience

Seeking Catherine (always Free!)

Seeking Fortune

Seeking Charity

Seeking Rachel

The Seeking Series

Oh Danny Boy

I Love You More

A Snowy White Christmas

A Portuguese Christmas

Holiday Hearts Book Bundle Volume One

Holiday Hearts Book Bundle Volume Two

Holiday Hearts Book Bundle Volume Three

Holiday Hearts Book Bundle Volume Four

Candleglow and Mistletoe

Maeve (Perfect Match)

A Christmas To Cherish

A Love Song To Cherish

A Valentine To Cherish

A Christmas Puppy To Cherish

A Homecoming To Cherish

Romance Stories To Cherish

Aloha to Love

Sweet Peppermint Kisses

Valentine Hearts Boxed Set

1-800-CUPID

1-800-CHRISTMAS

1-800-IRELAND

1-800-SUMMER

1-800-NEW YEAR

The 1-800-Series Sweet Contemporary Romance Bundle

Irish Hearts Sweet Romance Bundle

Holly's Gift

A Chocolate-Box Valentine

A Chocolate-Box Christmas

A Chocolate-Box New Years

A Chocolate-Box Summer Breeze

A Chocolate-Box Christmas Wish

A Chocolate-Box Irish Wedding

Chocolate-Box Hearts

Chocolate-Box Hearts Volume Two

Chocolate-Box Double Hearts

Recipes from the Heart

Leading Hearts

New Year Hearts

SENIOR HEARTS

A Summer To Cherish

Summer Hearts

Romance Stories To Cherish Volume Two

Cherished Hearts

Christmas in the Air

A Very Christian Christmas

The 1-800-Series Volume Two

The 1-800-Series Complete

Christmas Tails of the Heart

Most books are available in ebook, audiobook, paperback, Large Print paperback and Hardcover.

Many are FREE on Kindle Unlimited!

EXCERPT FROM 1-800-CUPID (A SWEET CONTEMPORARY ROMANCE)

Twenty thousand dollars.

Click.

Candee Contando licked her dry lips. She'd done it. She'd placed an online bid on a home-auction website for the Victorian mansion on Thompson Lane. Her dream home, her dollhouse. Her dilapidated project.

Two years of savings. Gone.

No matter. Under her guidance, she'd transform the mansion to its former majestic state, painted a mustard-yellow offset by ornamental burnt-sienna "gingerbread" trim. The sounds of children's giggling and music and barking beagles—yes, beagles—would echo across all five acres of the property.

She surveyed her offer and beamed, savoring the moment.

Now if she only could ensure that no one else bid on the property and drove up the price.

She studied the ticking clock on the website. Stay optimistic, she told herself. Deteriorated by age and wear, the Victorian would scare off any prospective buyer.

She pushed away from her desk and surveyed her real estate office. Although only one room, she prided herself on the cheery décor. One wall featured photos of North Carolina—the majestic peaks of the Blue Ridge parkway and scenic waterfalls. Below the photos hung a map of the area with local real estate listings highlighted by pushpins.

She peered out the window into the street below. Since noon, a bright sun had been at odds with January's wind—a wind crazy in its intent to blow the streetlights off their wires.

For the umpteenth time, she checked her nonringing cell phone for messages. Surely the real estate market in Roses, North Carolina, would improve. Didn't prospective home buyers begin looking in January? And wouldn't these buyers call her rather than her competitors? Candee prided herself on her professionalism and up-to-date listings.

Then why hadn't she made a single sale since August?

On the heel of that depressing assessment came a cheerful one. In two hours, she and her older sister, Desiree, planned to enjoy dinner at Desiree's country club.

Candee stepped back to her desk and switched off the computer.

Two single women in their late twenties, she mused, spending Friday night alone and dateless, four weeks before Valentine's Day.

Her cell phone rang, most likely Desiree firming up dinner plans and reminding Candee not to be late. Regardless of what time Candee met her older sister anywhere, Desiree always arrived before her.

Candee clicked on her phone. "1-800-Cupid," she said with a laugh.

"Contando Realty?" a man asked.

"Yes, yes ..." So much for professionalism. Candee felt her cheeks color. She hurried to her desk, dropping into the chair and switching her phone to speaker. "Are you looking to buy a home today, sir?"

"I am." The man hesitated. "Is this the correct number?"

She powered on her computer. "Absolutely."

"I'm new to the area and checked into the Roses Hotel last night," he said.

Envisioning the rundown hotel, Candy raised her eyebrows. Although in all fairness, the hotel was the only lodging open in the winter. Roses, North Carolina, was a summer tourist town known for bubbling hot springs and cool mountain temperatures.

Her fingers poised on the keyboard. "I'm more than happy to assist. Your name?"

"Teddy. Teddy Winchester." He had a deep voice, a slight southern drawl.

"What type of home are you searching for, Mr. Winchester?"

"The worst home in the best neighborhood."

Yup. It figured. No significant sales commission to pay the mortgage this month. Fortunately, her part-time job at the local hardware store was stable, although the pay was meager.

She scrolled through the listings. "For yourself, sir?"

"I'm an investor."

"How many bedrooms and baths?"

"Three bedrooms, two baths. Single family and one level."

"Budget?"

"Anything below $50,000."

She rubbed the back of her neck. *Who did he think she was, a miracle worker?*

End of Excerpt *1-800-CUPID* by Josie Riviera ***

Want more? Keep reading *1-800-CUPID.*